JR

D0407662

Too Much Drama

THE MOSTLY MISERABLE LIFE
OF APRIL SINCLAIR

Too Much Drama

LAURIE FRIEDMAN

MINNEAPOLIS

Darby Creek
A division of Lerner Publishing Group, Inc.
241 First Avenue North
Minneapolis, MN 55401 USA

For reading levels and more information, look up this title
at www.lernerbooks.com.

The images in this book are used with the permission of: iStockphoto.com/
PandaWild (smiley and sad face).

Main body text set in Janson Text LT Std 12/17.
Typeface provided by Linotype AG.

Library of Congress Cataloging-in-Publication Data

The Cataloging-in-Publication Data for *Too Much Drama* is on file at the
Library of Congress.
ISBN 978-1-4677-8589-1 (trade hard cover : alk. paper)
ISBN 978-1-4677-9570-8 (eBook)

Manufactured in the United States of America
1 – BP – 12/31/15

For Gloria Rothstein—a great
friend and reader!
—L.B.F.

Taking a new step, uttering a new word, is what people fear most.

—*Dostoevsky*

Sunday, November 30, 5:45 p.m.
In my room

Someone should invent a product, like a smoke alarm, that alerts you when a life disaster is coming your way. Say, when your best friend since kindergarten is about to show up, tell you the friendship is over, then make a dramatic exit to prove she means it. Because that's exactly what Brynn just did, and it would have been nice to be prepared.

Brynn came over after lunch, and she looked upset. I could tell she'd been crying.

She'd told me she was going with her parents to Birmingham to see her grandmother, who has been sick. They're really close, so I thought that was the problem. "Is Nana OK?" I asked when I opened the front door and saw the look on her face.

"Can we go to your room?" Brynn asked.

"Sure." I figured if she had bad news, she didn't want to share it with me on my front porch. When we got to my room, I closed the door. Brynn sat down on my bed. She was still crying. I handed her a tissue. "What's wrong?" I asked softly.

Brynn made a grunting sound and then got up and walked to the other side of my room. The way she did it gave me the feeling she didn't want to be sitting on the bed with me, but I thought for sure I was imagining things. There's been a lot of tension between us for a while, but right before her trip to Birmingham, Brynn had been supportive when I was nervous about the solo I performed in the dance show. It seemed as though we were back on better terms, and I didn't see what could have changed. "Did something happen?" I raised a brow to show I was encouraging her to explain.

Brynn shot me a piercing look. "You know what happened." She pressed her lips together as if she was waiting for me to respond.

I shook my head. I had no idea what Brynn was talking about.

"Don't play dumb," said Brynn. "It's insulting."

I didn't like where this was going. "What are you talking about?" I asked.

"Billy broke up with me," said Brynn. "And it's your fault."

"WHAT!" The word flew out of my mouth. I couldn't believe what I was hearing. I didn't know that they'd broken up, and the idea that I had anything to do with it was crazy. "What are you talking about?" I tried to keep my voice steady.

Brynn's voice was anything but. "Billy. Broke. Up. With. Me. And. It's. Your. Fault." Brynn enunciated her words like she wanted each one to sink in.

My shock was turning into anger. Brynn's

accusations were ridiculous. "I didn't even know you broke up. How could I have had anything to do with it?" I asked.

"You're supposed to be my best friend." Brynn's voice rose as she spoke. "And ever since Sophie moved to town, you haven't acted like it. You're always protecting her and taking her side. I get that she's your sort-of cousin, but you treat her as if she's some pathetic newcomer who can't take care of herself. You know as well as I do that she's liked Billy from the moment she moved to Faraway, and you haven't done anything to stop it."

Who did Brynn think I was? God? "What could I possibly do to stop how one person feels about another person?"

Brynn pointed her finger at me accusatorily. "See! You admit it. Sophie does like Billy. I knew it."

"Are you trying to trap me?" I asked. "I didn't admit anything. Whatever happens between Sophie and Billy has nothing to do with me."

Brynn shook her head from side to side like

she didn't agree. "You don't get what it means to be a friend, do you?"

Even though Brynn was the one who showed up mad, now I was too. "You're the one who doesn't get how to be a friend," I said. "When you and Billy started going out, you didn't even tell me. I had to hear it from other people. How do you think that made me feel?" I paused so I could gather my thoughts. There was a long list of things Brynn had done over the past few months that fell into the Bad Best Friend category. I'd held a lot in, and now I wanted her to hear all of it.

But I didn't make it any further down my list.

"I don't really care what you have to say," said Brynn. "I didn't just come here to tell you that Billy broke up with me."

This was complete insanity. "There's more?" I asked.

Brynn took a deep breath and exhaled loudly. "I came to tell you that our friendship is over. It's a shame, but you're not the girl you used to be."

I'd heard enough. "Neither are you," I said to Brynn.

She smirked. "What are you saying? That you don't want to be friends either?"

"That's exactly what I'm saying." I wiped my forehead. My room felt too warm.

"Great," said Brynn. "We finally agree on something. Then she walked toward my door as though she was leaving, but she stopped short and turned to face me. "You make me sick, April. You really do." Then she walked out of the house and slammed the front door behind her.

I heard her loud and clear, and I'm sure everyone else in my house did too.

6:01 p.m.

May and June just came into my room. "Mom wanted me to tell you it's time for dinner," said May. She gave me a tentative look as if she wanted to say something about what happened, but wasn't sure what. "I'm sorry Brynn yelled at you," she said.

"Thanks," I mumbled.

May opened her mouth like she was going to say more, then she shut it and left. It was clear my room wasn't somewhere she wanted to be. I couldn't blame her.

June didn't budge. "We heard Brynn screaming," she said. "I Googled it, and it's impossible for one person to make another person sick unless you poison them. You didn't poison Brynn. Did you?"

I laughed. "I didn't poison her." It was a ridiculous, albeit interesting, idea.

"Are you and Brynn still friends?" asked June.

I wasn't sure how to respond to that. But June didn't wait for an answer. "Tina Chen and Katie Cross were best friends in first and second grade, and now they're not friends because Tina is friends with Carson Brooks, who Katie doesn't like." June looked at me like it was my turn to comment.

Her grade-school analysis of friendship and its application to my situation was impressive. I smiled at her. "I don't really want to talk about this," I said.

June nodded like she understood. "Do you want to eat dinner?"

"That's exactly what I'd like to do," I told my little sister. I had no idea that breaking up with your bestie could give you an appetite.

Apparently, it can.

7:17 p.m.
Post-dinner

I love roasted chicken but not when it's served with a side dish of curiosity.

At dinner, Mom couldn't stop asking questions about what happened with Brynn. "Did you girls have a fight?" she asked as soon as we sat down.

"Mom." I stuffed my mouth full with chicken and rice and silently willed her to get that my lack of an answer meant it was a topic I didn't want to discuss.

But Mom's mind-reading skills were particularly weak tonight. "Did something happen at school?" she asked.

I chewed slowly, swallowed, and then took a

sip of water. "Lots of things happen at school," I said.

Mom made a face. "I meant did something happen between you and Brynn? At school or elsewhere for that matter?"

"April didn't poison her," said June.

I had to laugh. Mom failed to see the humor. "April, what is going on with you and Brynn?" She put her fork down and looked at me like she was waiting for an answer. She reminded me of the girl in *Charlie and the Chocolate Factory* who told her dad she wanted an Oompa Loompa, and she wanted one NOW!

"April doesn't want to talk about it," said June. For only eight, her voice was impressively authoritative.

Mom looked from June to me, and then, without saying another word, she picked her fork back up and took another bite of her dinner.

I winked at June to let her know she'd done a good job at managing the dinner conversation. June smiled back, looking pleased with herself.

But she couldn't have been half as pleased as I was to not be talking about Brynn.

8:17 p.m.
called Billy

Even though I didn't want to talk to my family about it, I had to call Billy to find out why he broke up with Brynn. I wasn't prying. I just needed to make sense of the way Brynn had acted. When I told Billy what happened when she came over, he was quiet for a long time while he thought about what he wanted to say.

"I broke up with Brynn because when I told her what you, Sophie, and I did last night, she freaked out. I told her it was no big deal, but she made it into one."

What Billy was describing sounded a lot like the way Brynn had acted earlier.

He kept talking. "I tried several times to explain that all we were doing was trying to help May. I told her why you called me to go TP-ing with you, and that June came along too. I explained that Sophie ended up coming along because it was something she'd never done before."

"That didn't work?" I asked.

"Nope." Billy kept talking. "Brynn accused me of waiting until she'd gone out of town to do something with Sophie. She even said you probably planned the whole thing when you found out she was leaving."

I guess that explained why Brynn thought this was my fault. "Did you tell her that when we finished at Krystal's house all we did was take my sisters out for ice cream?"

"Of course," said Billy. "But she said Sophie likes me, and I'm clueless to it. She said she always flirts with me. She even accused you of not doing anything to stop it."

I felt my anger resurfacing.

"She wouldn't stop," said Billy. "I told her to calm down, but that really set her off, so I hung up. I thought she would cool down and realize how irrational she was being, but she didn't. She called me back and started yelling again." Billy paused. "I don't know. It was too much, and I snapped. I told Brynn we were over."

Billy let out a breath.

Brynn knows as well as I do how much Billy hates confrontations. I'm sure the whole thing stressed him out. Still, I couldn't help feeling a little sorry for Brynn. I know how much she likes Billy. This can't be easy for her.

As Billy kept talking, I tried not to picture Brynn. I could see her, face down on her pale pink comforter, crying into the silk pillow cases her Mom brought her back from Paris when she turned ten. When Billy and I hung up, my instinct was to call her and make sure she was doing OK.

Old habits die hard, but after what happened today, it's time to make some new ones.

9:44 p.m.
Called Leo

When I hung up with Billy, I decided to call Leo, who's older and wiser. I mean, he's only sixteen, but it's not just an age thing. I knew he'd have an interesting perspective.

"Ending a friendship is like a form of death," he said when I told him what happened.

"It's normal to experience a feeling of loss."

I hadn't thought about it like that. "Do you think it's possible to be mad and sad at the same time?" I asked.

"Why not?" asked Leo.

"Hmm." I took in what he'd said. Then I paused, thinking about the fact that Leo is leaving in a month to go to college. "It's going to be weird when you're gone," I said. "What am I going to do if something happens and I want to tell you about it?"

Leo laughed. "The same thing you're doing now. Pick up the phone and call me."

10:59 p.m.
Reeling

I've never used that word before. *Reeling.* It sounds like it belongs in a bad romance novel or a documentary about fishing. I just can't believe my friendship with Brynn is over. Other than my family, she's been the most important person to me since I was five. It's hard to imagine my life without her in it.

Leo was right. It is kind of like a death.

I keep thinking about what Brynn said earlier—*I'm not the girl I used to be.* But Brynn isn't who she used to be either. I'm not sure when the problems started. She wasn't happy when Billy and I started going out, or when I made the dance team in eighth grade and she didn't, or when I told her I was dating Matt Parker. Maybe it was jealousy. Maybe it was something else. But she hasn't been much of a friend to me for a long time, and she's been mean to Sophie from the day she got here last summer. I don't know what to make of it or of the latest development. Should I be mad? Relieved? Resigned?

I think I'm going to have to go with *all of the above.*

Little girls are cute and small only to adults. To one another they are not cute. They are life sized.

—*Margaret Atwood*

Monday, December 1, 9:37 p.m.
Poor May

When May came into my room to "say goodnight," I knew what she was really doing was giving me the daily wrap-up, which (fortunately) was that she didn't have any problems at school with Krystal Connery. I know she was scared to go today because of what happened with Krystal on Saturday night. I can't blame her for feeling anxious. But here's the bottom line: Krystal deserved what she got.

It started when May kicked the winning

goal at the game on Saturday afternoon. Everyone in the stands went crazy screaming and cheering for her. I expected May to be flying high after the game. But she was quiet as we piled into the car and didn't say a word all the way home. It took some coaxing when we got home, but she finally told me what happened.

"After the game, we had a team meeting," said May. "When it was over, Coach Newton left. Everyone was getting their stuff together, just kind of hanging around and some of the girls told me how awesome I played."

I was confused. "That's a good thing, isn't it?"

May shook her head from side to side. "That's when Krystal said I look like a boy and should play on the boys' team."

"It's kind of a compliment that she thinks you're good enough to play with the boys," I said.

"She said I *look* like one," said May.

She started to tear up, and my big-sisterly instincts kicked in. Even though May comes off as strong on the outside, she's ultrasensitive, and Krystal has been mean to her since soccer season started. Krystal was the star player until May waltzed in (or I guess I should say, kicked her way in), but that doesn't give her the right to be a bully. "You can't let her do that to you," I told May.

"What am I going to do?" she asked.

I shook my head. "It's what *we* are going to do." I got Billy on the phone, told him the problem, and we both agreed it was time for our favorite prank. It had been a long time since we'd done it, and I knew he'd want to help. "We're going to TP Krystal's house, and you're coming with us," I told May.

"No way!" said May. "What if Krystal sees me?"

"Well you usually don't want the person to see you, but in this case, you do."

"Why?" May asked.

"You want her to know you did it, so she won't bully you anymore."

"What if this makes it worse?" May asked.

"It won't."

May looked skeptical.

"You have to show her she can't mess with you. Trust me?" I asked.

May finally nodded, so Billy and I made a plan to TP Krystal's house that night. When I mentioned to Sophie what we were doing, she said she wanted to come too. "I've never heard of rolling a house in toilet paper," she said. "No one did that in Paris or New York. Although maybe that's because most people live in tall buildings that would be hard to cover."

"You don't actually cover the house." I tried to explain to Sophie the process of how you throw the toilet paper up and over trees and bushes. She said it didn't make sense, but she was excited to see it.

So Saturday night, Sophie and Billy came over, and we planned to take May to Krystal's house as soon as it got dark. But as we were filling my backpack full of rolls of toilet paper, June came into my room. "Where are y'all going? What's that toilet paper for?" she asked.

May shot me a look like she didn't want June to be part of this, but it gave me a great idea. "We're going to have to say something to Mom and Dad about where we're going," I said to May. "If we take June, we can tell them we're all going for ice cream." I shrugged. "It's what we're planning to do anyway after we're done at Krystal's."

June eyed the rolls of toilet paper. "Whatever you're doing, I want to go," she said. She looked excited.

May crossed her arms across her chest. "I wouldn't have gotten to do something like this when I was her age."

"Beauty of being the youngest," said June like it was already decided she was coming along, which I guess it was. I was pretty sure Mom and Dad wouldn't approve of me teaching my little sisters how to roll a house, but they'd be happy I was taking them both for ice cream.

So we all left for Krystal's house. When we got there, Billy and I showed Sophie, May, and June how to throw the rolls up high over the branches of trees so that the toilet paper would hang down on both sides. Sophie tried throwing a roll up into a tree a few times but gave up because she wasn't very good at it. Neither was June. May, on the other hand, was great.

"You're a natural!" said Billy.

Even though I know May was scared out of her mind, it was easy to see she was as proud of her rolling skills as she is her soccer skills.

Normally when we roll a house, Billy and I wear all black and don't say a word. But since the whole point was that we wanted Krystal to hear us, we were laughing and talking as we rolled.

"What if Krystal's parents come outside and we get in trouble?" asked May.

"When Krystal hears the commotion, trust me, she'll be the first one out of her house," I said. I knew there was a chance that might not happen, but fortunately, it did.

Krystal came outside a few minutes after we started. "I see you!" she said.

May started to panic. "C'mon!" she said. "Let's go!"

But I motioned for May to follow Billy and me. Sophie and June came too. We walked, with May in tow, right up to where Krystal was standing on her front porch. Billy was the self-appointed spokesperson. "Was there a problem on the soccer field today?" he asked, looping an arm around May.

Krystal looked slightly horrified, like she might vomit. "I don't know what you're talking about it." But clearly, she knew exactly what Billy was talking about.

Billy gave Krystal his best fake politician smile (which is very good). "I heard there was a problem," he said gesturing to May. "And I want to make sure there won't be anymore. Understand?"

Krystal nodded.

"Great!" said Billy. Then he handed Krystal a half-used roll of toilet paper, and we left. As May, June, Sophie, Billy, and I walked to the Cold Shack for ice cream, we were all in good moods.

"You sounded like a mobster," said Sophie.

We were all laughing as Sophie imitated the way he'd talked to Krystal. When we got home, May came into my room and thanked me. I was happy having done something to help my sister. I think Billy and Sophie were too. I can't help but think that it's really sad and pretty stupid that what started with a backpack full of toilet paper and a desire to help May led to all the problems with Brynn.

10:32 p.m.
Thinking about Brynn

I didn't know what would happen at school today, after my "breakup" with Brynn yesterday. The good news is that not much did.

I saw Brynn, dressed in black, looking morose, but she didn't look at me. In fact, she looked everywhere but at me. I was worried all day that it would be awkward when we got to dance practice. I guess I should be grateful to Ms. Baumann, who by chance put us in different groups.

I don't know why, but I keep thinking about the play kitchen Brynn had in her room when she was little. I can still picture it perfectly. It was light pink and yellow, and it had an oven, stove, refrigerator, and cabinet all built in. I thought it was beautiful.

When we were in kindergarten and first grade, we'd make pretend tea parties with all the little dishes and plastic foods. As we got older, we'd play restaurant and make up menus and elaborate dishes. We named our restaurant Choco-Cherry. I never liked the name, but Brynn said we were at her house, so she got to pick it.

Brynn also got to decide which dishes and foods we would use and what we would put on the menus we made. I remember telling her one day that I wanted to decide what we would serve, and she told me that's not how the game was played. I went along with what she wanted, and we kept playing.

I'm sure I thought it was no big deal then, but Brynn was always the one in charge. This sounds very high school English class, but I think it's a metaphor for the demise of our friendship. It worked as long as I played by Brynn's rules.

I guess it has just taken me a very long time to come to that realization.

10:47 p.m.
Text with Sophie

Sophie: Can I wear the sweatshirt you left at Gaga's?

Me: Why would you want to?

Sophie: I love it.

Me: It looks like a dishrag.

Sophie: I'm wearing it inside out.

Me: Sounds worse than right-side out.

Sophie: It's super cute!

Me: You can have it.

Sophie: You'll want it back.

Me: It's yours.

Sophie: It has your name in it.

Sophie: Literally. Camp name tag I think.

Me: 😊

Sophie: 😊

I couldn't help smiling as I put my phone away for the night. Sophie could easily be the kind of person who is intimidating—she's beautiful and sophisticated, and she speaks fluent French. But then she does little things, like taking an old sweatshirt and turning it into something she thinks is cute and then wanting to give it back to me because she thinks I'll like it. Stuff like that makes her easy to be friends with.

I don't want to name names, but not everyone belongs in that category.

Something's wrong.

I didn't get my way.

—*Glinda*, Wicked

Wednesday, December 3, 7:48 p.m.
In my room
Bad day at dance

Brynn showed up to school this morning wearing all black, and dark sunglasses between classes, for the third day in a row. She was making a statement. I ignored it all day, but when we were in the bathroom in the gym changing for dance, she was actually making moaning sounds like she was in pain.

I felt I had to ask. "Are you OK?"

"Obviously not," she said. Then she looked

at me like it was physically painful to be in the same room with me. "You know you're the last person I feel like talking to." She paused, letting her words sink in. When she continued, her voice was lower like she wanted only me to hear what she was about to say.

"I'm going to apologize to Billy for what happened. I don't really think I did anything wrong, but I know he was upset." She paused again. "I'm the kind of person who is willing to take responsibility when I do something that upsets someone else."

The implication was that I wasn't. I didn't even bother to defend myself.

Brynn continued. "Billy just needed some time," she said. "I'm sure we're going to end up back together. I thought you should know."

It was my turn to say something, but what could I have said? *Good luck. I hope it works out. Keep me posted.* There was nothing I could say that she'd want to hear. I pressed my lips together in silence.

Apparently, Brynn interpreted my silence as smugness.

"You know, just because you went out with Billy first doesn't mean you know him better than I do." She scrunched her face up as she talked, which made her eyes seem smaller but wider than usual. She looked like a garden snake. "I guess you've forgotten that the reason he broke up with you is because you cheated on him." She practically spat the words at me. Then she turned and walked out of the bathroom.

And the award for most unlikeable former best friend goes to . . . Brynn Stephens.

9:42 p.m.
Text from Sophie
Sophie: Do you have an elf hat?
Me: Fresh out.
Me: ???
Sophie: It's for the assembly.
Me: Still fresh out.
Sophie: I'll have to make one.
Me: Why don't you ask Santa to bring you one?
Sophie: No time. Need it tomorrow.

Me: Wish I could help. Sorry!

Me: ☹

Sophie: Gaga to the rescue. She has green felt.

Sophie: ☺

Thursday, December 4, 1:17 p.m.
Study Hall

Brynn is in the WORST MOOD.

I've been sitting here trying to figure out why. I thought maybe it had something to do with the assembly this morning.

SGA put on a skit to remind people to bring in toys for the holiday toy drive. Billy was Santa, Marcy Franklin was Mrs. Claus, and the rest of the student government reps were elves. Nothing happened in the skit that should have upset Brynn. I could see why she'd be mad if Sophie had been Billy's fictional wife, but that role went to Marcy, who is not only a senior but has also been dating Jeff Ingraham, another senior and SGA president, for the last two years.

I don't know why Brynn's so upset, but she's sitting two rows in front of me, and I can literally sense her bad mood from where I'm sitting. She keeps grabbing notebooks out of her backpack and shoving them back in. She actually grunted at one point, got up, and threw a mechanical pencil in the trash. I guess she pushed so hard she broke it.

The study hall monitor, Ms. Cunningham, asked if she was OK. Her response:

"Great, just great."

Which means she's anything but.

9:52 p.m.
Talked to Billy

Now I know why Brynn was in such a foul mood, and for a change, it wasn't because of anything I did. Billy told me that after the assembly, Brynn went up to him and asked if they could talk.

He told me Brynn said she was really sorry about what happened and wanted to know if they could get back together.

"What did you say?" I asked Billy.

"I told her I couldn't talk about it right then because I only had four minutes to change out of my Santa suit before my next class."

I knew there was nothing funny about the situation, but I couldn't help smiling at the image of Brynn trying to have a serious conversation with Billy while he was wearing a red suit and fake beard.

"What happened next?"

"She told me we didn't need to talk about it and that it was a simple *yes* or *no*. I told her it wasn't that simple, and she got mad." He paused. "I was standing there dressed like Santa, trying to get to my next class on time, and she was yelling at me about how I'm selfish and don't care about her feelings. Everyone who walked by was looking at us like we were crazy."

It sounded like a scene from a bad movie. I would be laughing if I saw it on TV, but unfortunately, it really happened.

"So what did you do?"

"I told her we were done. Then I walked off, changed clothes, and went to class."

That explains Brynn's bad mood.

10:07 p.m.
Considering things from another perspective

I don't want to keep thinking about Brynn, but I'm having a hard time not thinking about her. How do you just stop thinking about someone you've been best friends with since kindergarten? Even though I've had it with her, we've been friends so long, I feel like I should try to put myself in her shoes.

She's mad at me because she thinks the problems with Billy started when Sophie moved to town. She thinks Sophie likes Billy, and I didn't do anything to stop it. But the truth is that even if Sophie does like him, what am I supposed to do? Tell her to feel differently? Refuse to be friends unless she changes her mind?

Brynn knows it doesn't work that way, so it's kind of unfair that she's mad at me because of how Sophie might (or might not) be feeling.

For that matter, how does Sophie feel about Billy? And vice versa? When Sophie first moved here, Billy was really sweet about her being the new girl. He introduced her to a lot of people, especially during the Student Government campaign, which I have to admit was a little surprising since he was running against her.

It was even more surprising that Sophie ran for SGA. In her old school in New York, she'd never done anything like that. I know how upset Brynn was when Sophie and Billy were elected as the ninth grade reps.

But still, just because Billy was nice to the new girl or they do the same activity doesn't mean they like each other. Honestly, I think a big part of Brynn's issue is that Sophie is so pretty. Brynn is too. She has a body like a model. But there's something special about Sophie. A lot of people would say it's her long dark hair and pale skin. But I think what makes her so threatening to Brynn is that Sophie's so interesting and different.

So if I'm looking at this from Brynn's perspective (which given how she's acted lately, isn't easy to do), I get why she's worried. Billy broke up with her, and she thinks it's because of Sophie. Still, that doesn't give her license to act like a crazy-jealous person.

OMG! I think I'm overlooking a critical point. Maybe Brynn isn't acting.

Sometimes the smallest things take up the most room in your heart.

—Winnie-the-Pooh

Friday, December 5, 7:57 p.m.
Pondering important questions

I keep wondering why Billy broke up with Brynn. I mean, I know why he said he broke up with her. But I wonder if there's a little more to it. Does he like Sophie? And for that matter, does Sophie like Billy?

I was asking myself those questions all afternoon, and with good reason.

After school, Sophie and I went to watch May's soccer game. Mom and Dad had told me earlier in the week that neither of them were going to be able to go, so I'd planned in advance for Sophie to come with me. I hadn't told anyone else we were going, which is why I was surprised when Billy showed up.

"Hey," I said. "How'd you know May had a game?"

"Sophie told me," he said as he sat down beside her. He passed us the bag of peanuts he had. I took a handful, cracked one open and popped it in my mouth. Then I looked at Sophie.

"I must have mentioned it at the SGA meeting this morning." She shrugged like it was no big deal. But as she dug into the peanut bag, I noticed she blushed a little.

An awkward silence settled between the three of us, and I felt like it was my job to fill it up. "I'm glad you came," I said to Billy.

He seemed relieved I'd said something, and turned his attention to the game. "Wow! May is really good," he said as we all watched her dribble the ball down the length of the field.

"It's hard to believe we share the same DNA."

Billy laughed. "I didn't say it!"

But we both knew that's what he was thinking. Other than dance, I've always been the last one picked to play on any team.

As we watched the game and ate peanuts, we joked around about my lack of ball-handling skills and the fact that Krystal, who had seen us sitting in the stands, hadn't given May so much as one dirty look today, even when May kicked her second goal of the game.

But as Billy and I laughed and talked and ate, I noticed Sophie was staying quiet. When she finished munching, she brushed the stray shells from her lap and then tucked her hair behind her ears. She shook it loose, then tucked it back again like she couldn't decide which way it looked better. It was weird because she's almost never quiet, and she's always confident about the way she looks.

We all cheered when May's team won the game. Then Billy said he had to go. When he told us bye, Sophie thanked him for the peanuts.

"Sure," said Billy.

"Seriously, they were really good," Sophie said. "I love peanuts."

Billy smiled at her. "Me too."

"Cool," said Sophie, like it meant something that they both like peanuts. I wanted to raise my hand and say I like peanuts too, but I didn't.

While we were waiting for May to finish her postgame team meeting so we could walk her home, I brought up what happened. "You were kind of making a big deal about the peanut thing. It seemed like you were acting a little weird around Billy," I said.

"I was?" Sophie's hands flew to her cheeks. She was blushing again.

"No big deal." It wasn't, and I didn't want her to be self-conscious. "I don't know, I guess it made me wonder if you like Billy." I bumped my shoulder lightly into hers and tried to keep my voice sing-songy. "I mean, do you?" Finally, the question was out.

"Of course I like Billy," said Sophie. "Everyone likes Billy."

I raised a brow at her. She knew what I meant, and that wasn't it.

I cleared my throat and tried again. "I guess what I'm asking is if you like him in a different way than everyone else?"

Sophie laughed. "That's impossible for me to answer. I don't know how everyone else likes him." It was the first thing Sophie had said all day that sounded like Sophie.

She hadn't answered my question, but the answer seemed pretty clear.

11:03 p.m.

I can't sleep. I can't stop thinking how weird it will be if Billy and Sophie end up together. First, I went out with him at the beginning of eighth grade. Brynn was next, this past summer. Then Sophie? Technically there's nothing wrong with it, but it just has that weird, backwoods, all-in-the-family sort of feel. Plus, there's no telling what Brynn will do if they start going out. She might implode. Or explode. Or go away to boarding school. I can't be sure. Aside from my own experience, I have no idea what people do when their ex starts going out with someone else. Actually, I do. It happens all the time on TV, and it can get pretty ugly. OK. I'm getting way ahead of myself here. Sophie hasn't even said she likes Billy. Oops, correction.

Everyone likes Billy.

Saturday, December 6, 10:30 p.m.
In bed
Mentally replaying my day

Leo called last night and asked me if I wanted to go holiday shopping today. I hadn't seen him since he came to watch me dance my solo the night of the dance show. But I love to shop for the holidays, so I told him I'd love to go. Plus, it seemed like a great use of my day, as opposed to thinking about the Brynn-Sophie-Billy triangle.

So Leo came to pick me up this morning, which was pretty exciting because it was going to be the first time I'd been anywhere alone with a boy in a car. I didn't want to make it seem like a big deal, and I was hoping Mom and Dad wouldn't think it was either. What I was really hoping was that by the time he came to get me, Mom and Dad would be long gone. But somehow they both picked this morning to get a slow start.

When Leo came inside to say hi to Mom and Dad, they were having coffee at the kitchen table. When I told them what we were doing, they thought it was a huge deal that Leo would be driving us to the mall.

"How long have you been driving?" Dad asked.

"Have you had any accidents or gotten any tickets?" asked Mom.

I was very irritated and more than a little embarrassed that my parents were grilling Leo about his driving habits. "Leo has a license," I said. "Do you ask everyone who has a license how long they've been driving or if they've had accidents or tickets?"

Mom and Dad both shot me a look that said they didn't like my attitude but didn't want to say anything that would embarrass me in front of Leo. I guess I should be grateful for that. I gave Leo a tell-my-parents-you-know-how-to-drive look, but he handled the situation in his typically unique and highly effective fashion.

"I completely get why you'd be worried," he said. "There's nothing scarier than teen drivers." He paused and looked at my parents. "Of course old people behind the wheel and black bears on the loose are pretty scary too."

Mom and Dad both laughed. I smiled too. It was hard not to appreciate Leo's attempt at humor.

"I'm a very careful driver," said Leo. His face had turned serious. "One of my greatest accomplishments is that in my first nine months of driving I've had no accidents and gotten no tickets. But I woke up this morning thinking about how hard it's going to be to find a parking spot at the mall during the holiday time."

Mom and Dad both nodded like they understood that.

"I don't want to inconvenience either of you," said Leo. "But if you have time to drop us off, I'd be happy to leave my car here. Or we could take the bus," he said looking at me. I nodded like that was fine, even though that was definitely not how I'd pictured our day.

"You don't need to take the bus," said Dad. "I'm leaving for the diner now, and I'd be happy to drop you off."

"And I can pick you up later when I close the store," said Mom.

"Great!" said Leo as he followed Dad to the garage. I was too shocked to speak. I never thought my first car date (if this was a date, which I wasn't even sure of) would include my parents, but Leo was totally cool with it, and it made me not mind so much. Leo chatted with my dad on the way to the mall and with my mom on the way home. I liked how comfortable he seemed around my parents.

But that wasn't even what I liked most about the day. There was a whole string of little things that Leo did.

When we were shopping for a scarf, he asked the sales lady if she thought aqua or peach was a better color for him. He held two scarves up to his face like he couldn't decide. The lady told him he was looking at scarves for women. The way she said it was condescending, like either he didn't know what department he was in or he did know and was making a questionable choice.

Some people would have gotten embarrassed or felt stupid, but not Leo. He told her that he's always thought a scarf seemed liked a fairly unisex product but that he happened to be looking for his mother, who has the same coloring he does. When she pointed to the aqua scarf, Leo very nicely thanked her for her help even though she'd been pretty rude to him.

And when we were walking to the food court to get lunch, Leo suggested we stop in the candy store on the way.

"Doesn't dessert come after a meal?" I asked.

Leo grinned. "It's the holidays—let's live large," he said as we sampled the peanut butter fudge on the counter.

"That's really good," I said. Leo agreed, and he asked the guy working behind the counter if we could take another sample.

"Sure," he said. He seemed surprised Leo had asked.

"Thanks," Leo said as he handed me a piece of mint fudge and took one for himself. Then he told the guy that he works in a deli and that his pet peeve is when he puts out a plate of samples and someone stands there eating them all.

"I know what you mean," said the guy.

He thanked Leo and wished us a happy holiday. As we left the store, I was thinking how much I liked how polite Leo was to everyone, especially at holiday time.

But I guess the thing that really stuck in my mind was what happened when I was buying mittens for May and June.

As I was looking through the piles of mittens and slipping my hands into pairs I liked, I couldn't help noticing that Leo had gotten quiet and was staring at me. It was kind of embarrassing. "What are you looking at?" I asked. The words sounded harsh, and I wanted to reel them back in as soon as I'd said them.

But Leo didn't seem to mind my question. He just answered it honestly. "You have pretty hands."

I'd never thought of my hands as anything other than functional, so I liked the thought that I could add "nice hands" to my list of good features. Then, to my surprise, Leo took my hands in his and inspected them. "Really nice mitts," he said.

The way he said it made me laugh. It was a reference to a baseball catcher's mitt, and I couldn't help but think of all the times Matt Parker had said stuff about baseball when we were going out. Most of what he had to say was about how he was good at it. It usually left me feeling cold and thinking that the main thing he liked talking about was himself. Leo's reference had the opposite effect—I felt all warm.

And I don't think it had anything to do with the mittens.

In the book of life,

the answers aren't in the back.

—Charlie Brown

Monday, December 8, 6:05 p.m.
Babysitting

I'm sitting on the couch with May and June, watching SpongeBob, eating Domino's, and thinking about my hands. The ones Leo said were pretty. I'm still kind of hung up (in a good way) on that comment. I'm also hung up (in a bad-phone-joke way) on why he hasn't called since we went shopping on Saturday.

Is he busy getting ready to go to college in January? He said he had a lot to do, but still, I would think he'd have time to make a phone call. I have no idea what someone has to do to get ready to go to college. It must be very time consuming.

Here's an idea: I'm going to call him and find out.

8:30 p.m.

Calling Leo was a good move. As soon as I called, he said he was sorry he hadn't called and that the reason he hadn't is because his grandparents showed up yesterday for a surprise visit. "One of the drawbacks to being an only grandchild is that when they come to visit, I'm the one they want to visit with," he said.

"Do you like your grandparents?" I asked.

"Yes," said Leo. ". . . and no. They're intense."

"What do you like best about them?" I asked.

"They like to talk to me about science, which I like talking about. My grandpa is a physicist, and my grandma is a neurosurgeon."

"I see why you're a chemistry genius. It must be genetic," I said.

"Quite possible," said Leo.

"So what do you like least about them?" It seemed only fair to ask.

Leo laughed. "What I like least is that when they come to visit, they don't like me spending my time with anyone but them." Then he told me he had to go but promised he'd call tomorrow night, as soon as his grandparents leave.

Tuesday, December 9, 10:02 p.m.
In my room

Leo called. But it's a shame he called when he did. I must have seemed distracted, because he asked if I had something on my mind, which I did, and we spent the whole call (which only lasted six minutes) talking about what happened in dance today.

The worst part is that it was so stupid, and talking about it made me seem stupid. I had told Leo about the recent drama with my friends on Saturday when we went Christmas shopping. So tonight I told him how Emily came up to me during our break at dance and said Brynn told her it was my fault that Billy broke up with her.

"What did you say?" Leo asked.

"I asked her what exactly Brynn had told her. She said Brynn said she should ask me why I would do something like that." I described how she put her hand on her hip and looked at me like I owed her some kind of explanation. "It had nothing to do with Emily," I said.

"Hmm," said Leo. "That sounds pretty complicated."

"Right?" I was glad he got it. "I mean, it was wrong for Brynn to drag her into it. Don't you think?"

"Yeah," said Leo. I waited for him to make one of his insightful comments about how silly it was that Brynn was bringing other people into something they had nothing to do with, but he didn't. "April, I'm not very good with girl stuff," he said. Then he told me he had to go. After we hung up, I looked down at my phone.

If it had a do-over button, I would have pushed it.

Not-so-secret Santa

My problems with Brynn are getting worse
by the day. She's going person-to-person on
the dance team and dragging them into her
warped thinking that I caused the breakup
with Billy.

I know this because today we were drawing
Secret Santa names, and when Vanessa Mendez
picked, she looked at me, which I was pretty
sure meant she drew my name. I also saw
Brynn, who was standing next to Vanessa, look
over Vanessa's shoulder and frown, which made
me doubly sure Vanessa had picked me.

Then after dance, Vanessa came up to me
and said Brynn told her I caused the breakup
with Billy. It was the same thing that happened
with Emily.

"I didn't cause any breakup," I said. "How
could I do that?"

What I'd meant was that one person can't
make another person break up with someone
else, but that wasn't how Vanessa took it.

"Exactly," said Vanessa. "When Brynn told

me, I said the same thing. How could April do that?" She paused and looked at me like she was waiting for her words to sink in and then continued. "I get that Sophie is kind of like family to you, but we're a team, and we're supposed to be a family. Maybe you should apologize to Brynn," she said.

"Sure," I said to Vanessa.

"Great," said Vanessa, like she'd done her job.

As I walked home, I was thinking two things.

One: there's no way I'm apologizing to Brynn. Two: Vanessa doesn't know sarcasm when she hears it.

Friday, December 12, 5:58 p.m.
It's a wrap
In more ways than one

Today after school, SGA had a wrap party for the toys they collected from the toy drive, and Sophie asked me if I'd stop by and help wrap. Everyone on SGA brought in Christmas cookies, and a bunch of kids were coming to help wrap. We didn't have dance practice, so I was happy to pitch in.

Apparently, so were Emily and Vanessa.

I was kind of surprised they came. They've both made it pretty clear they're allies with Brynn on the breakup issue. They know Billy is on SGA, so I would have thought it was an event they would boycott in support of Brynn.

But as we started to wrap gifts, I started to get paranoid that they came *because of* Brynn. I couldn't help but wonder if she'd sent them as spies. They were both watching Billy the whole time. He and Sophie stood side by side wrapping presents, eating cookies, and laughing, and Emily's and Vanessa's eyes were glued to them.

Billy's always a comic, but today when he told a joke, his friend Jake Willensky said, "Dude, that's the dumbest joke," and a couple of kids actually booed and gave it a thumbs-down sign. No one thought it was funny—except Sophie. She actually put her head back and laughed out loud like she thought it was hilarious.

I hadn't meant to, but when she started laughing, I looked in Vanessa and Emily's direction. It was pretty obvious they had taken note of Sophie's reaction, because when I looked at them, they were both looking at me. Vanessa rolled her eyes, and Emily shook her head. Neither of them said anything to me, but they didn't have to.

I knew exactly what they were thinking.

9:02 p.m.
Looking for answers

I was sitting on my bed thinking about everything that's happened lately with Brynn and Billy and Sophie and Leo and even the girls on the dance team, and my brain filled up with questions.

Are Billy and Sophie going to end up together? How will Brynn react? What's going to happen with the girls on the dance team? Is Brynn going to try to turn them all against me? Will it work? And what about Leo? Do I like him as more than a friend? Does he think about me that way? What's going to happen when he goes to college?

Those were just some of the questions

bouncing around in my brain when May came into my room and wanted me to help her with her math homework.

"It's Friday night," I reminded her. "You have until Monday morning."

"I know," said May. "But I have a soccer tournament all weekend." She put her book down in front of me. "Please, April. I'm really confused. I could use some help."

I groaned. I wasn't in the mood to do math. "You know, the answers are in the back of the book," I said.

May shook her head. "Just the odd ones. What do I do about the other problems?"

"That's hard," I said. But I wasn't just talking about math. It's life in general. Friends. Boys. Relationships. There are always lots of questions.

But not nearly enough answers.

If we did all the things we are capable of, we would literally astound ourselves.

—Thomas Edison

Saturday, December 13, 3:30 p.m.
Annoyed

Today Mom had to be at her store all day, and Dad took May to her soccer tournament, which meant I was stuck at home babysitting June. It shouldn't have been a big deal. The plan was that she would read while I studied for my Bio test. But June had other plans in mind. "We should bake Christmas cookies," she said.

I don't love to bake, but it's better than studying Bio. "Sure," I said.

So June and I congregated in the kitchen, and she read the recipe while I got out the ingredients and started mixing things together. We stirred red and green M&Ms into the dough, and I had just put the tray in the oven when my phone rang. It was Leo.

"I have to get this," I told June.

"What about the cookies?" She looked alarmed.

"Don't worry," I mouthed to her after I'd said hello to Leo. I walked to my room and shut my door. I hadn't spoken to Leo since Tuesday when I'd told him about the drama in dance and he'd said he wasn't good with girl talk. It wasn't our best talk, and I wanted this one to be better. "What's up?" I asked in a cheerful voice.

"I spent the morning slicing five pounds of ham, six pounds of turkey, and four pounds of roast beef," he reported. Then he told me he has twelve days left of work, which means if he slices approximately fifteen pounds of meat each day, he will be retired from the deli business "in exactly one hundred and eighty pounds."

"Of meat?" I asked.

"Of meat," Leo confirmed.

I giggled. "What's it like slicing all that meat?" I asked Leo.

He cleared his throat and was talking in an authoritative sounding voice. "That depends on which meat you're talking about."

I sat back on my bed and listened as Leo talked about the different slicing challenges inherent in ham and turkey. He'd just gotten to roast beef when June barged into my room. "April, the cookies are burning!" she said.

"I have to go!" I told Leo. I dropped my phone and raced to the kitchen, but it was too late. The Christmas cookies June and I had baked were black.

"Crap!" I said as I took the tray from the oven.

"You're not supposed to swear," said June. She looked like she was about to cry.

"I'm sorry," I said.

"About burning the cookies or swearing?" asked June.

"Both."

"Can we make more?" June asked.

"Not now." I told her. I really had to study. "Maybe Dad will help you bake some more when he gets back after the tournament."

June seemed content to wait. But it was a mistake to tell her to wait for Dad to bake more, because when he got home, she told him that we baked cookies, and I let them burn.

"April, that's not like you to allow cookies to burn," said Dad when he came into my room after June told him what happened. It was annoying that he'd decided to read into why I'd let the cookies burn.

"It wasn't a big deal," I said glancing up at him from my textbook.

But Dad seemed to think it was a bigger deal than I was letting on. "Was there something on your mind?" he asked.

"Yeah," I said. "Biology." I didn't think I needed to share with him that it wasn't the only thing on my mind.

"April, I know you and Brynn have had some issues lately. You've been friends for a long time. Why don't you try talking to her?"

Dad paused like he was debating if he wanted to say more, but I beat him to the punch. I really didn't want to get into a whole conversation about Brynn with him. "Dad, I really need to study."

"OK," he said. "Focus on school."

"I'm trying to," I said. I was proud of myself for not saying that it would be a whole lot easier to do that if he'd stop trying to talk to me and go.

But before Dad left my room, he gave me a look. "April, I'm always here if you want to talk."

"Thanks, Dad." I appreciated that he wanted to help. There have been lots of times when talking to Dad has been helpful. But I didn't feel up to it today. I don't know if I was annoyed by the topic or by Dad's prying.

Probably a little of both.

Monday, December 15, 4:45 p.m.
Went to a study session
Didn't do much studying

It's exam week, and today was a study day. Since we didn't have to go to class, Billy,

Sophie, and I decided we'd all study together for our English test tomorrow.

We met at Billy's house, and we were sitting at his kitchen table, studying our vocab words, but it was hard to focus.

We were trying to think up mnemonic devices to help us remember the meanings of words. Billy was great at it. When he grows up, it could be his job. He'd get rich quick thinking up funny ways to remember the definitions of words.

For *supercilious*, which means arrogant, he came up with super silly ass. (For which his mom called him by his full name and gave a disapproving look. "No, like a donkey!" he said, although I don't think his mom was convinced.)

For *remiss*, which means careless, he made "miss" jokes. *I missed what you said. I missed my bus. I'm so careless I missed dinner.* When he said the joke about missing dinner, he clutched his stomach and moaned like he really was hungry. Sophie literally collapsed into a heap of laughter, which made Billy laugh too. As I sat there watching, it was pretty obvious there's a lot of chemistry between them.

I'd be remiss not to notice.

How's that for a mnemonic?

Wednesday, December 17, 10:17 p.m.
Talked to Leo for an hour

Leo called tonight while I was studying. "I can't talk," I said. "I have an Algebra test tomorrow."

"I can help," said Leo. "I love Algebra."

"It's impossible to love it," I said.

Leo laughed. "Algebra helps us understand and make sense of the unknown."

"That makes no sense," I said. Leo and I spent the next half hour debating the merits of Algebra, although I doubt that will help me on the test.

Once we'd said everything there was to say on the topic (at least in my opinion), somehow we started talking about the fact that he's leaving for college in less than three weeks. He told me about the classes he's taking and the dorm he'll be living in and about his roommate, who is from China. Then Christmas came up, which made me think about Brynn.

I told Leo that even though she's been a jerk for a while, I feel kind of sorry for her about the whole Billy thing. "She was my best friend for a long time," I said. "It's the holidays, and I feel like I should try to reach out to her. I'm just not sure what to do. She's made it pretty clear that she doesn't want to be friends."

"Why don't you invite her to yoga," suggested Leo.

I smiled at the memory of the day Leo took me to yoga.

"I don't think it's Brynn's thing." I paused. I was thinking about Leo, not Brynn. "I like that you always have a unique solution for things."

"That's me," said Leo. "Mr. Unique Solutions."

I laughed. "I was being serious. You always have good ideas."

"Are you surprised?" asked Leo. He sounded like he was offended.

"No, but you did say you're not good with

girl issues." I paused. "You seem pretty good to me."

"I guess you never know what you're good at until you try," said Leo.

Thursday, December 18, 4:40 p.m.

My last exam was today. It was Algebra, which I have with Brynn. My seat is right behind hers. When she came into the room, she sat down and never turned around. I finished my test early, and after I turned it in, I spent the rest of the time looking at the back of Brynn's head and wondering . . . What goes on inside it? I thought about what Dad said— that I should try to talk to her. But when the test ended, Brynn got up and walked out of the room. She never even looked at me.

What do you say to that?

Friday, December 19, 3:07 p.m.
Dance team holiday lunch

I just got home from Pizza Hut where the dance team met for lunch and to exchange Secret Santa gifts. Brynn had drawn Emily's name. I watched as Brynn gave Emily a spa bath set and then as Vanessa gave Brynn a Chia pet. There's no way Brynn would like that gift, but she acted like she did.

I could say a lot of negative things about Brynn, but one of her best qualities is that she loves giving and getting gifts. No matter what she gets, she's always gracious and happy about it. Brynn and I have always made a big deal over exchanging Christmas gifts, and it made me wonder if Brynn has even thought about getting me a gift this year. That's when it occurred to me that I hadn't gotten her anything, but I should. It was the solution I was looking for. It's probably bad holiday karma not to be speaking to your former-long-time best friend.

Even worse not to get them a gift.

> *The only way to have a*
> *friend is to be one.*
>
> —*Ralph Waldo Emerson*

Sunday, December 21, 10:02 p.m.
Gaga dropped a bomb

Gaga has done a lot of unexpected things over the years, so whenever she does what my Uncle Drew calls her "crazy thing," I'm never all that surprised. But I was shocked tonight at dinner when she announced that she and Willy had booked a last-minute cruise and wouldn't be with us for Christmas. I wasn't the only one who was shocked. I thought my mom and her sisters might go into cardiac arrest at Gaga's dining room table.

"Mom, you can't leave us at Christmas," said my mom. She sounded like a two-year-old.

"I already have tickets," said Gaga.

"But Christmas together is our family tradition," said my Aunt Lilly.

"And we always have it at *your* house," said Aunt Lila. She made a face like she was a puppy that had been left outside in the rain.

Willy took Gaga's hand and gave it a squeeze. I guess they'd anticipated this reaction, and he was silently reminding her to be strong. "You will be just fine without me," said Gaga.

Everyone stood there, speechless. Finally, my little cousin Izzy broke the silence. "Are you still going to give us presents?" she asked.

"Of course," said Gaga. She smiled at Izzy and her twin, Charlotte, who were both started clapping and rambling on about how much they like presents.

Then she turned her attention to the grownups at the table who were all looking at one another like they had a real problem on their hands. "For goodness sakes," said Gaga.

"Your silence is worse than your screaming. Stop being so dramatic and eat your meatloaf."

So we did. At least some of us did. Aunt Lila took a tiny bite and made a face like Gaga's news had killed her taste buds. Aunt Lilly used her napkin to wipe her forehead.

"She's premenopausal," my cousin Harry announced to the table.

Amanda laughed out loud.

Aunt Lilly shot a stern look to both her kids. She told Harry that even though he's almost an adult, he wasn't acting like one, and that certain topics need to stay in the privacy of their home. She said we could do Christmas at her house, and she got up and went to the kitchen for a legal pad. When she came back, she started making her to-do list.

Christmas should be interesting this year.

Monday, December 22, 4:15 p.m.
Back from the mall

I rode my bike to the mall. I'd been debating all weekend about what to get Brynn, and I still couldn't decide. I didn't want it to be too personal or too impersonal. Just something nice to let her know she's still important enough to me to give her a Christmas present.

I also didn't want to pick it out with anyone else. Mom and Dad have both tried talking to me about what's going on with Brynn since the day Brynn screamed we weren't friends anymore. I know they're worried, but I just don't feel like talking to them about it, so I didn't want them to drive me there.

I didn't want Leo to go with me either. I'd already told him that I wanted to get her a present, and his suggestion was to take her to yoga. Even though he hasn't said it, I think he thinks all the drama with her is silly. But still, it's there, and I can't just ignore it.

And I didn't want Sophie to go with me. She's not a fan of Brynn. She'd probably want to know why I'd get Brynn a present after how she's treated me. She wouldn't be wrong. But Brynn and I have a history.

So I went by myself, and after a full day of shopping (I've never bought an ex-best friend a Christmas gift before), I got her cinnamon-scented bubble bath and body lotion. That sounds kind of anticlimactic, given how much thought I put into it. But Brynn loves bath products. And the smell of cinnamon.

I think it's perfect.

10:17 p.m.
Text from Sophie
Sophie: My dad comes tomorrow.
Me: Are you excited to see him?
Sophie: IDK.
Sophie: Kind of weird he's coming to Faraway.
Me: I'm sure it'll be fine.
Sophie: He's staying at the Faraway Inn.
Me: Might not be fine.
Sophie: Ha ha.
Sophie: Not what he's used to.
Me: They have an indoor pool.
Sophie: ☺
Sophie: Christmas will be weird.
Me: Presents are never weird.
Sophie: That's true.
Me: When do you leave for New Orleans?

Sophie: Day after Christmas.

Me: Sounds like fun!

Sophie: It will be!

Tuesday, December 23, 8:45 a.m.

Awake

The first things I saw when I opened my eyes were the presents I got for Brynn. The bottles of bubble bath and lotion were on my dresser, just standing there, silent and unwrapped.

If they could talk, they would have been saying: *When are you going to give us to Brynn, and what are you going to say to her?*

For a couple of mute bath products, they ask all the right questions.

1:35 p.m.

Billy called

I was going to go to Brynn's this afternoon and give her the gift, but Billy just called and asked if I wanted to go on a bike ride.

Bike ride with Billy versus awkward moment with Brynn.

That's a no-brainer.

When Billy and I stopped at Mr. Agee's farm, where we always stop for our rest break, we got on the subject of Brynn. It was kind of weird that she wasn't on the ride. The three of us always took bike rides together. Plus, she's the one who always brought the drinks and snacks. That sounds a little cold, like I only wanted her there because we were hungry and thirsty, but that wasn't the case.

"Do you miss her?" I asked.

Billy nodded. "I called her and told her I really hope we can be friends," he said.

"What did she say?"

"She said she doesn't want to be friends."

"That was it?" I asked.

"That was it," said Billy.

I gulped. If she told Billy she didn't want to be friends, I could only imagine what she's going to say when I give her the bubble bath and lotion.

I have a feeling it might not be "Merry Christmas."

When I woke up this morning, I decided to just do it. I got dressed, ate a banana, and went to Brynn's house to give her the gift. I wasn't sure what I was going to say. I figured the right words would come.

Her mom answered the door. "I have a Christmas present for Brynn," I said. I held out the wrapped bath products to Mrs. Stephens.

I was a little self-conscious. Brynn's mom is a perfectionist, and the package looked like I'd wrapped it myself. Plus, I realized I had no idea what Brynn had told her mom about what happened. I'm sure she'd told her mom that Billy broke up with her, and I wouldn't be surprised if she told her that she thought I'd had a hand in it.

Mrs. Stephens frowned. I felt my stomach drop.

"Brynn will be so disappointed she missed you," said her mom. I couldn't tell if she meant what she was saying. "Brynn went to run an errand with her dad, but she has a gift for you too." Mrs. Stephens half closed the door and walked away. When she came back, she had an elegantly wrapped box in her hands. "This is for you," she said. "Merry Christmas, April."

I exchanged boxes with Brynn's mom and told her to tell Brynn I said *Merry Christmas*. As I walked home, I thought about how uncomfortable the exchange had been. I'd been to Brynn's house hundreds, maybe thousands, of times. Lots of those times I'd gone inside without knocking, and today Mrs. Stephens didn't even invite me in.

When I got to my room, I opened the gift from Brynn. It was a bottle of Donna Karan Green Apple perfume. I've had a bottle of it sitting on my dresser for the last two years. It's shaped like an apple, and it's pretty hard to miss, which means Brynn either deliberately got me something she knew I already had, or she didn't even bother to get me a gift and let her mom pick it out.

Either way, the gift said it all.

I will honor Christmas all the year,

and try to keep it in my heart.

—*Charles Dickens*

December 24, 11:15 a.m.
Feeling down

I keep thinking about what happened this morning when I took the gift to Brynn. It's depressing. This is what you're supposed to do during the Christmas season:

A.) Forgive.

B.) Forget.

C.) Move on.

Apparently, Brynn decided to go with:

D.) None of the above.

1:45 p.m.

Not so down

Leo just called and said he's bringing over gifts for me, which greatly improved my mood.

"Did I hear a plural?" I asked.

Leo laughed. "That's for me to know and you to find out."

"Well I have something for you too," I said.

"Singular?" Leo asked.

It was my turn to laugh.

"I'm leaving now," said Leo. "See ya."

It was the least articulate but possibly most exciting thing I'd ever heard come out of Leo's mouth.

4:45 p.m.

Was I ever down?

I just had the most amazing Christmas Eve afternoon with Leo and not just because he brought me gifts. He's the most unique person I've ever known. When he came over, I answered the front door. He asked if I wanted to open my presents, but he didn't have anything with him. "Where are they?" I asked as I looked around.

"Start looking," said Leo.

"Huh?" I was confused.

"You'll have to hunt them down if you want them," said Leo.

"I think you might have your holidays mixed up." I gave him a questioning look. "Isn't that an Easter thing?"

Leo laughed. "If you want your gifts, you're going to have to find them." So I starting searching around my porch, in the bushes, under a pile of pine needles in my yard, and even in the mailbox. "Cold," said Leo.

I shook my head like I was giving up. Leo grinned and held out his hand, and I took it. It was the first time we'd held hands, aside from when he inspected my hand while we were shopping. It felt a little awkward as we walked to a little wooded area in the park where he said my gifts were waiting. But once we got there, the awkwardness was replaced with excitement. There were three boxes wrapped in bright red paper, and they weren't hard to find.

"April, you have a real talent for sniffing out presents," said Leo once I'd collected all my boxes.

We sat side by side on a bench as I opened my presents. The first one was a silver duct tape wallet with a red duct tape heart on the front. "I made it," said Leo.

It kind of looked like he had, but I loved that he'd obviously put a lot of time and thought into what he gave me. "It's great! I can't wait to use it," I said.

The next present was a book called *Chemistry for the Non-Chemist.* "I hope it doesn't bore you to sleep," said Leo. He looked a little embarrassed about the gift he'd chosen. "I thought you might like knowing a little bit about my favorite subject."

"I can't wait to read it," I said. "And I'll also be a step ahead of most people when I take chemistry next year."

Leo grinned. "I'm glad I gave you a dual-purpose present." Then he handed me the third box. I peeled off the wrapping paper and inside the box was a little porcelain figurine of a ballet dancer. "I know you're not strictly a ballerina," said Leo. "But she kind of reminded me of the way you looked when you danced your solo in the dance show."

I studied the slim statuette of the ballerina with her hair pulled into a bun. She was so beautiful. I'd like to believe that's how I looked the night of the dance show. It was pretty cool to know that's how Leo saw me that night.

"Do you like it?" asked Leo.

"I love it," I said sincerely.

When Leo smiled at me, I could see that he was blushing a little. "Merry Christmas, April."

"Merry Christmas, Leo."

As I said the words, he bent over and kissed me on the cheek. "Now where's my gift?" he asked.

"Hiding," I said as I recovered from his unexpected move. We got up and started back to my house. We held hands again, and this time it felt comfortable as we walked and talked.

When I gave him the clock I had gotten him for his dorm room, I was a little embarrassed. "My gift is kind of boring compared to what you got me."

"April, this is the best gift you could have gotten me. You have probably noticed that punctuality is not my strong suit."

Actually, that was not something I'd ever noticed. "I got you the clock because the lady at the store said it's something everyone who is going to college needs. You're never late when we have plans," I said to Leo.

"I guess it's easy to be on time when you're showing up for something you like," said Leo. I tried to think what activity he meant—yoga? Walking? It took a minute, but then the intent of his words sunk in.

It was my turn to blush.

Christmas Eve
At home

Tonight we celebrated Christmas Eve at home. It was just supposed to be Mom, Dad, May, and June and me. But my Uncle Marty called my dad this morning and said Sam was supposed to go with his mom for Christmas, but the plans changed, so Uncle Marty and Sam drove from Mobile to Faraway to spend Christmas with us.

We ate the delicious dinner Dad made: grilled lamb chops, twice-baked potatoes, asparagus, and homemade strawberry cheesecake. Then we opened presents. When we were done, Mom told June she should sleep in May's room so Sam and Uncle Marty could have her room.

"Do you have one bed or two?" Sam asked June.

"One," said June.

Sam shook his little head from side to side. Blond bangs flopped into his eyes. "I'm not sleeping with Daddy," he said. "He farts in his sleep."

"Sam! I don't like that word," sad Uncle Marty.

"Daddy poots in his sleep," Sam corrected. "And it stinks." He held his nose and made a retching sound. May, June, and I cracked up.

"Girls, that's enough," said Mom. I knew she didn't want us to egg Sam on, but I guess

June couldn't help herself. "What does it smell like?" she asked Sam.

"June!" said Mom.

"Dog poo," said Sam. He collapsed into a heap of laughter.

"Sam! That's enough," said Uncle Marty. His tone was sharper than before. Everyone but Sam got that it was time for him to stop.

But Sam was just getting warmed up. "If he farts when Santa comes, Santa will be grossed out by the smell and won't leave any presents."

"Santa won't leave presents for little boys who say *fart*," said Uncle Marty.

I knew he was teasing, but apparently Sam didn't. He started crying. He was wailing that he was sorry and wanted his presents. He was actually apologizing to the air, like he wanted Santa to hear his words even though he wasn't there. It was the saddest thing I've ever seen.

Even Uncle Marty felt bad. He told Sam he was kidding and let him have a second piece of cheesecake. Sam sniffled while he ate it. When he finished, Uncle Marty said it was his bedtime, but Sam said he was still upset and scared too. So we all stayed up watching the Santa report on TV until Sam fell asleep in Uncle Marty's lap.

For some reason, watching Uncle Marty carry Sam to bed later made me emotional. Maybe it was that Sam looked so small and sweet. Or maybe it was just the contrast of how bad I felt this morning when I tried to give Brynn the gift I'd gotten her versus how good I felt tonight celebrating with my family. It was a surprisingly fun night all being together. It made me wish I could take the holiday spirit I'm feeling and sprinkle it all over Brynn.

Sadly, I don't think it would make a difference.

Christmas, 10:17 p.m.

We spent Christmas at Aunt Lilly and Uncle Dusty's house. I thought it would be weird not having it at Gaga's and even weirder that she wasn't there to celebrate with us. Even though I missed Gaga, Christmas was very merry!

May was the first one to wake up (she always is), and she got everyone else up. All our stockings, and one for Sam, were laid out in the den in front of the fireplace. They're always filled with pretty much the same thing—candy, socks, and little things from the drug store, but I still love opening mine and seeing what's inside. Sam liked his too. He stuffed his candy and socks in his underwear, then put his stocking on his head and wore it around like a hat. We all ate homemade cinnamon rolls for breakfast, and then everyone got dressed and we went to Aunt Lilly's house.

My whole extended family was there. Aunt Lilly, Uncle Dusty, Harry, and Amanda. Aunt Lila, Uncle Drew, and Charlotte and Izzy. Uncle Marty and Sam. There was a huge tree, and every room was decorated for Christmas. Mom, Aunt Lilly, and Aunt Lila all had on the matching Christmas sweaters Gaga had made for them.

Sophie was there too, with both of her parents. I know she'd been worried that it would be uncomfortable. It was the first time they'd all been together since Sophie and her mom moved to Faraway. But as soon as we all showed up, Aunt Lilly made everyone put on the Christmas hats she'd ordered and sing carols while she played the piano. I guess singing in funny hats loosens people up, because everyone seemed relaxed after that. Then we ate the huge lunch Aunt Lilly had made and opened presents. It was a really fun day.

When we got home from Aunt Lilly's, Uncle Marty and Sam left to go back to Mobile, and it was just Mom, Dad, May, June, and me. I think we were all exhausted from last night's and today's festivities. We all went into the den, and Mom and May and I curled up on the couch, and June sat with Dad in his oversized armchair. We watched some cheesy, made-for-TV Christmas movie, but it was nice just being with my family.

When the movie was over, Mom made us all get up and get ready for bed.

I showered and had just gotten into bed when Mom came into my room. She walked over and sat down on the edge of my bed. She looked at me like maybe there was something

on her mind she wanted to talk to me about.
But all she said was, "I love you."

"Love you too," I said to Mom and gave her
a big, goofy smile. Mom laughed, kissed me
on the forehead, and left. As I watched her go,
I realized I wouldn't have changed one thing
about the day.

Some days, every once in a while, are perfect.

Only do what your heart tells you.

—*Princess Diana*

Friday, December 26, 8:45 a.m.
Post-Christmas blues

The day after Christmas is always a letdown, but I'm feeling it more than usual this year. Sophie is leaving for New Orleans with her dad, Billy is in Mexico with his family, Leo is getting ready to leave for college, and I'm not friends with Brynn anymore, which leaves me with a question.

What am I going to do for the rest of the break?

10:45 a.m.

Text from Sophie

Sophie: At the airport.

Sophie. Leaving for NOLA!

Me: Have fun!!!

Sophie: What are you doing this week?

Me: Nothing much.

Me: ☹

Me: Hurry home!

Sophie: Miss you already!

Me: ☺

1:32 p.m.

Text from Billy

Billy: Merry Christmas! How was it?

Me: Fun. How's Mexico?

Billy: Nice! Bobby and I are going skiing this afternoon.

Me: Water or snow?

Billy: Did you really just ask that?!?

Me: Just kidding. Is it hot there?

Billy: Very!

Me: Have fun!

Billy: Thanks.

4:42 p.m.

Text to Sophie

Me: Did you get Kaitlin Reed's invite?

Sophie: Let me check.

Sophie: OMG!

Me: I can't wait.

Sophie: Me too!

Me: When are you home?

Sophie: 12/31!

Me: You better get back in time!

Sophie: Flight lands at 2.

Me: What if it's late?

Sophie: I'll take a bus.

Sophie: Or walk.

Me: That's a long walk.

Sophie: I'll hitchhike.

Me: Bad idea.

Sophie: I'll be back in time.

Sophie: I promise!

Sophie: I'm not missing that party.

Me: 😊

Sophie: 😊

Saturday, December 27, 10:59 p.m.
Fun night

Leo called this afternoon and invited me to go to a movie with him tonight! He picked me up, and this time Mom and Dad let me ride with him there. But we didn't go to the big theater behind the mall. We went to an old theater in downtown Faraway that was restored a few years ago. I'd never been in it, but Leo said he loves it. It shows art films.

The lobby of the theatre was really pretty. Everything was dark purple and gold, and there were fancy antique mirrors on the walls. The concession stand looked old fashioned, but fortunately it had normal snacks.

Leo and I agreed we'd each pick one thing and choose one together. I picked popcorn, Leo got Milk Duds, and we agreed on a Diet Coke.

Once we had our snacks, we found seats for the movie, which was an Italian film called *Cinema Paradiso* that I LOVED! Leo had seen it before—it's actually one of his favorites. It was about this guy who is a filmmaker. It's

told in flashbacks, so you get to see the story
of what happens to him while he was growing
up. He goes through a lot, but at the end, he
makes peace with his past, which a) gave me
tremendous hope for the future, and b) made me
cry like a baby because it was so sweet and sad.

Leo had brought tissues—he said it's
common to get a little misty-eyed at that
movie. Part of me thought it was a little weird,
because the only other person I know who
goes to movies with tissues is Gaga.

But as we drove home and talked about
the movie, I realized I'd had such a good time
tonight that I really didn't care that the boy I
like has something in common with my eighty-
year-old grandmother.

Did I just admit I like him?

I think I did!

Sunday, December 28, 7:15 p.m.
A day with Mom

I spent the day with Mom at her store doing
inventory. I learned a lot about clothes and
costs, but I think Mom learned more about me.

"How about some lunch?" she asked after we'd spent the morning counting and folding. "You could pick up sandwiches from the deli next door." She winked when she said it.

I pretended not to notice the wink, but I took her up on her suggestion. I knew Leo was working, and I was happy to have a reason to go.

"April!" said Leo as soon as I walked in. "I'm thrilled you stopped by."

"You're that excited to make me a ham sandwich and a turkey sandwich?" I asked teasingly.

Leo laughed. "I'm always happy to make you a sandwich. I was going to call you later. Tomorrow is my last day working at the deli, and I was wondering if you could spare some time on Tuesday to go shopping with me. I need some new clothes for college, and since you're the daughter of a fashion designer, I'm hopeful you're genetically predisposed to having good taste."

"I'm not bad," I said. I'd give both Brynn and Sophie higher marks than me in the fashion department.

Leo laughed. "Well whatever you pick will be better than what I'd get myself."

I smiled at him. "I'd love to go," I told him.

"Great!" said Leo. When he finished making the sandwiches, I paid and took them back to Mom's store.

"Someone looks happy," said Mom when she saw me.

I tried not to grin, but I couldn't help it. "I like hanging out with Leo," I told Mom. Then, I don't know why, but I confided in her that I'm a little anxious about what's going to happen when he leaves for college.

Mom unwrapped her sandwich. "You'll figure things out. Just enjoy spending time with him while he's still here," said Mom.

I unwrapped my sandwich and took a big bite. I'm not so sure how I'm going to "figure things out." But like it or not, in less than a week, that's exactly what I'm going to have to start doing.

Today Leo and I went shopping, and then I went back to his house with him to help him pack. It was the first time I'd been to his house. The entry hall, living room, and dining room were filled with artwork and antiques, which was why I was surprised when I went to Leo's room. It was so plain. White walls. Blue bed. A little shelf with a few knowledge bowl trophies on it.

"I know you're wondering why there's nothing on the walls," said Leo.

I tried to read his expression. I couldn't tell if he was embarrassed or acknowledging the obvious. I didn't want to lie. But I didn't want to tell the truth either, which was that I *was* wondering why his room was so bare. I remained motionless.

Leo explained, "I like it like this. It gives me space to think."

I thought for a minute before I responded. "There's always so much going on in your head. It makes sense that you don't need much on your walls," I said to Leo.

Leo seemed relieved. He put down the shopping bags he was holding and walked over to where I was standing. Then he bent down and kissed me. It wasn't a long kiss. Just a sweet, small one. It was nice, but it was followed by a long, awkward silence.

"I like you, April," said Leo.

"I like you too," I said.

I waited to see if Leo was going to elaborate on what liking me meant, but he didn't. I don't know what he was thinking, but what I was thinking is that he's leaving for college in less than a week. "I don't want to sound like the voice of practicality here . . . but how's that going to work with you gone and me here?" I asked.

"I'm not sure," said Leo. "But there's always a solution—it's just a matter of finding it."

"This isn't a chemistry experiment," I said.

Leo smiled. "It kind of is." He had a point, but it wasn't an answer to my question. Maybe Mom was right when she said we'll figure things out.

But how?

10:15 p.m.

Phone call from Leo

Leo called tonight to ask if I wanted to do something on New Year's Eve.

I told him about the invite I got from Kaitlin Reed. "It's going to be a really fun party. All my friends will be there, and I'd love for you to hang out with them. Why don't you come?" I was sure Leo would say no.

But he surprised me. "I guess I'd better go to my first high school party before I go to my first college party."

"This isn't really your first high school party, is it?" I asked.

"Technically, it's my second." Leo laughed. "But it's a date, and I can't wait."

That makes two of us.

If you love someone, set them free. If they come back they're yours; if they don't, they never were.

—Richard Bach

New Year's Eve
Pre-Party

I've spent a large part of today on the phone.

I talked to Dad twice. The first time he called from the diner (while I was sleeping) to remind me that I'm babysitting today and that Mom is closing the store early and will be home by four. I went back to sleep, but he called a few minutes later to tell me to make lunch for May and June. Since Mom won't be home until closer to dinner time, I didn't really think I needed that reminder, but in the holiday spirit of things, I said no problem.

I talked to Mom once. She called after lunch to tell me she'd be home at four and to make sure I'd made lunch.

I've talked to Sophie five times, which is how many times it took for us to decide what we're each wearing to Kaitlin's party tonight. In my case, it's a minidress with wedges, and Sophie is wearing a miniskirt with a cropped sweater and boots.

And I talked to Leo once to give him the address of Kaitlin's party so he can meet me there. I'm going to walk to Gaga's to get Sophie, and then we're walking together to Kaitlin's house, which is just a few blocks from where Gaga lives.

Finally it's party time, and I'm off! (As in, off to the party, versus off the phone. But I'm that too.)

Still Pre-Party

I'm not off just yet.

I was about to leave when Dad saw my outfit (which I'd spent the better part of my day planning) and stopped me.

"Not so fast!" he said. "You can't go out in those shoes. You'll freeze."

"Dad, it's 40 degrees, which makes it physically impossible to freeze, and I'll be inside most of the night." Dad wasn't convinced, so now I'm wearing a minidress and boots. As I said before, I'm off! But this time I mean it.

Post-Party
A lot to write about

It's New Year's Day, so HAPPY NEW YEAR! Sophie slept over after the party and she just left, so I feel like I should write about last night and finish the year out before I start writing about the new one.

Kaitlin decorated her house with tons of black, gold, and sparkly New Year's Eve stuff she bought. Her brother and dad hung twinkly lights in the trees in the backyard, and her mom made amazing food. Her brother's best friend was the DJ and played great music. Everyone was dancing, and it was really fun.

I'd been a little worried all day about Leo,

but he had a great time too. He's not a great dancer—actually, he's pretty bad—but he gets an A for effort, and he looked like he was having fun when we danced.

We spent a lot of time just hanging out with my friends, especially Billy and Sophie. They were asking Leo all about going to college. I could tell he felt good that they thought it was cool he's smart enough to be going at sixteen.

As it got closer to midnight, Kaitlin was giving out hats and shakers and blowers and glow sticks. When the clock struck twelve, everyone was screaming and going crazy. I had a blower, which I blew into Leo's face. "Happy New Year!" I said.

Leo laughed and took the blower out of my mouth. He had a New Years hat on that he put on my head and said, "Happy New Year, April!"

Then he leaned over and kissed me. I was surprised he'd kissed me at the party, and I looked at him to see if I could figure out what he was thinking. It was hard to read his expression, and it would have been weird to just stand there looking at him, so I looked around the room.

I guess part of me was looking to see if anyone had been watching us. The party was packed with people, and I don't really think anyone cared what Leo and I were doing. But as I looked, I saw Sophie, who was standing next to Billy, turn and kiss him on the lips. It wasn't a quick kiss like the one Leo gave me. And Billy kissed her back. And unfortunately, I wasn't the only one who saw it.

I looked at Emily and Vanessa, who were standing nearby, and I saw that they were watching too. Vanessa saw me watching her, and made a face like what she'd just witnessed wasn't something that should have happened. Then she leaned over and whispered something to Emily, who turned and looked at me.

I looked at Brynn, who was standing next to Vanessa and Emily. Her back was turned to Billy and Sophie, so I knew she hadn't seen the kiss. But I also knew that she would definitely hear about it from Vanessa and Emily. The only question was when.

I got an answer to that question before I

left the party. Vanessa and Emily cornered me when I came out of the bathroom. "We're telling Brynn," said Vanessa.

I didn't have to ask what she meant. "Why would you do that?" I asked.

Emily made this weird, high-pitched sound. "Brynn deserves to know that Sophie is going after Billy."

"Don't you think that's going to upset her?" I asked.

Emily rolled her eyes. "Obviously."

"Sophie should have thought of that before she kissed Billy," added Vanessa.

I didn't know what else to say to Vanessa or Emily. Sophie kissed Billy, but he didn't exactly *not* kiss her back. They know as well as I do that Billy isn't going out with Brynn anymore. He's free to kiss whomever he wants.

I felt sick as I thought about what Brynn will do when she finds out. I wanted to ask when they were planning to tell her and suggest that a good time would be after we graduate. But I knew it would be a whole lot sooner than that.

When the party started to die down, I told Leo good-bye, and Sophie and I left. As we were walking home, Sophie linked her arm through mine. "I like Billy," she said. There it was—a delayed response to the question I'd asked at May's game. She looked so happy. And oblivious.

I didn't want to upset her, but she had to know what happened with Vanessa and Emily outside the bathroom. As I told her, her smile disappeared. "It's no one's business if I like Billy. If Emily and Vanessa get involved, it's just stupid, small-town gossip."

It was the first time I'd ever heard Sophie say anything negative about Faraway. "I'm sorry," I said. "I had to tell you." I paused. "I don't know what Brynn will do."

I could see Sophie's frown, even in the dark. "Brynn doesn't own Billy," she said. "It's a free country. He can like whoever he wants."

"True," I said. "Billy can do what he wants."

I didn't say this, but so can Brynn.

New Year's Day
Disaster strikes

Dad closed the Love Doctor Diner today and had a brunch there for my extended family, which should have been great because Dad makes the best brunch. Ham, bacon, cheese grits, scrambled eggs, biscuits, and homemade cinnamon rolls.

Unfortunately, Mom decided (without asking me) to include Billy's and Brynn's families. "Mom, how could you do that?" I asked. I put my empty juice glass down on the kitchen counter. Granted, Mom didn't know what happened last night at the party, but she's aware that Brynn and I aren't speaking to each other. "I don't see how you could invite the Stephenses. It's going to be so uncomfortable."

"They have been family friends for a long time," said Mom.

"That's not a reason to invite them, especially without asking me."

"April, it's a new year," said Mom. "You and Brynn should both be able to put aside whatever is happening between you and get along for a few hours."

I knew the matter was closed. Mom couldn't uninvite them. But as I got dressed to go to the diner, I felt the orange juice I'd drunk churning in my stomach. I didn't know if Vanessa and Emily had told Brynn yet about what happened, but I literally felt sick thinking about it.

The bad feeling I had about how the day would turn out grew as my extended family filtered in. By the time Sophie and her mom arrived, and then Billy and his family, I had a sinking feeling about what was going to happen. Unfortunately, it turns out my intuition was spot on.

I saw Brynn's face as she walked into the diner, and I knew she'd heard what happened at the party. She went straight up to Sophie. She hugged her and whispered something in her ear. I could tell from the way Sophie recoiled that whatever Brynn had said to her wasn't as sweet a greeting as it seemed.

Brynn looked at Billy, but she didn't say

anything to him. Then she walked toward me and gave me the same hug she'd just given Sophie. "I hate you," she whispered in my ear. Her words sounded more like a threat than a statement.

My eyes found Billy's. We've been friends for so long I think he understood that there was a problem. He walked over to where Brynn and I were standing and looped his arms around both of us. To everyone else, I'm sure it looked like a friendly gesture. He steered us outside and motioned for Sophie to follow.

"What's the problem?" he asked when we were finally out of earshot. I didn't say anything, and neither did Sophie.

"You're disgusting," Brynn said to Sophie. She practically spat the words at her.

"OK, calm down," Billy said. Even though he didn't look in Brynn's direction, I knew it was meant for her. "We can figure this out."

Billy loves diplomacy as much as he hates confrontation. I knew his intention in bringing all of us outside was to clear things up. I also knew it wasn't happening.

"Everyone saw you kiss Billy at the party," Brynn said to Sophie. "I guess you don't care about your reputation."

"Brynn!" said Billy.

Sophie looked hurt. "You and Billy broke up," she said.

Brynn moved away from Sophie, like being anywhere near her was physically unpleasant. She turned her attention to Billy. "You're so pathetic," she said.

Then she looked at me. "And you're nothing. You're absolutely nothing to me, and you never will be." Then she put her hand on her head and went back inside and said something to her mother. A few minutes later the Stephenses left.

Not a great way to start the new year.

Hope smiles from the threshold

of the year to come, whispering,

"It will be happier."

—*Alfred Lord Tennyson*

Friday, January 2, 9:15 a.m.
Waking up

I woke up this morning to Mom sitting on the edge of my bed. "What happened yesterday outside the diner? Carol called this morning, and she's concerned about what's going on with you and Brynn. So am I."

The last thing I wanted was for the moms to get involved. Sleepiness was my only weapon. I closed my eyes. "Mom, I'm not even awake yet. I don't want to talk about this."

But Mom wasn't letting it go. "April, I

know you and Brynn have had some issues,
but you, Billy, Brynn, and Sophie were outside
talking yesterday. and you all looked upset. Did
something happen?"

There was no way I was telling Mom about
Sophie and Billy kissing or what happened
at the party with Emily and Vanessa. "Don't
worry," I said. I yawned like I was going back to
sleep. "It'll all work out," I mumbled.

But I'm not so sure it will.

Saturday, January 3, 10:45 p.m.
Saying good-bye

Leo is leaving for college tomorrow, so
tonight we had what he called our *last date*.
"It's kind of ironic," he said. "We just had our
first date, and we're already on our last." He
laughed. I could tell he thought he was being
pretty funny.

I would have laughed too, but it felt like I
was having a lot of "lasts" for so early in the
year. I couldn't help thinking about Brynn.
New Year's Day was probably the last time I'll
ever speak to her.

As I thought about it, my mood darkened.

"Penny for your thoughts," said Leo as we sat down with plates of chicken and rice and hummus from the Middle Eastern restaurant in the food court at the mall.

In the short time I've gotten to know Leo, I've learned there's no point in not telling him what's on my mind, since he seems to get when something's troubling me. I told him what happened at the diner. "Brynn is being so unreasonable. How can she hold me responsible for what happens between Sophie and Billy?"

This wasn't the first time we'd discussed this. I knew Leo's opinion on it. He thinks Brynn is lashing out at me when the real issue is between Brynn and Billy (why they broke up) and between Billy and Sophie (if they're going to get together.) "You don't even belong in this fight," he said. "You've tried to be a friend to Brynn," said Leo. "But it takes two."

I nodded. It was a pretty simple way of looking at things, but it's the truth. "I get why you're upset," said Leo, sensing I wasn't quite done with the topic. "Brynn was your BFF for a long time."

I giggled. It was funny to hear BFF come out of his mouth.

He smiled. "I know what a BFF is," he said and continued. "I think the only thing you should be asking yourself is if you did everything you could to try to talk to Brynn and be a friend to her."

"I did. But she was so mad at the diner. I've never seen her confront someone like that. Who knows what else she'll do when school starts again?" Something tells me she's not getting over this so fast.

Leo dipped a pita chip into the little pile of hummus on his plate and stuffed it into his mouth. He chewed and swallowed, then looked at me. "Why worry about tomorrow today?" he asked. "Especially when today is our last day to hang out for a while."

He had a point. "Why don't we talk about you?" I said.

"The only topic I like talking about less than other people is myself," said Leo.

I wasn't letting him off the hook that easily. "You're leaving for college tomorrow. How do you feel?" I hadn't meant to sound like I was interviewing him, but that's how my question came off.

"Scared," Leo said honestly. He paused. "My mom was the one who thought I should go to college, but my dad never did. He thinks I'm too young. I broke the tie, so now off I go. I know Tuscaloosa is only a few hours away, but it feels like I'm going to New Zealand." Leo shrugged. "I hope it's the right decision."

I felt like I needed to boost his confidence. "You'll do great," I said.

Leo nodded like he appreciated my faith in him. "But there are a lot of things I'm going to miss," he said.

"Like what?" I asked flirtatiously.

Leo laughed. "Like you, April."

"Good answer!" I told him.

We left the food court and walked around the mall and talked. He drove me home, and I sat in his car for a long time in my driveway before I got out. I didn't want to say good-bye, but it was getting late.

When it was time for me to go in, Leo leaned across the seat and kissed my cheek. It was sweet, but sad. Then he told me he had a final good-bye gift for me. "I'll send my first-ever text to you when I get to campus."

"I'm honored," I said.

"I really *am* going to miss you," said Leo.

"Me too," I said.

"You're going to miss you too?" asked Leo. "But you'll be here with yourself every day, whereas I, on the other hand, won't see you until I return home in February." I knew he was teasing. The absurdity made me laugh even as I was telling him good-bye. Somehow, whenever I'm around him, I'm happy.

Even when I'm sad.

Sunday, January 4, 8:45 p.m.
Last night of winter break

Going back to school at the end of a break is always stressful, and I'm not the only one who thinks so. May and June just came into my room. June pointed to May. "She's nervous about going back to school tomorrow." Even though I felt bad for May and it was kind of funny to see June in the role of junior spokesperson, I wasn't in the mood to deal with my little sister's problems. I had my own issues to deal with.

June didn't wait for me to ask for an explanation. "May is trying out for the softball team and so is Krystal. We might have to TP her house again."

I bit my lip to keep from smiling. "You can't go around throwing toilet paper in people's yards every time they're mean to you," I said.

"See?" May said looking at June. Clearly they'd been discussing this.

"So what's the issue?" I asked May.

She brushed a stray hair off her face. "I guess I'm just scared about tryouts."

"You're such a good athlete. You'll make whatever team you try out for," I said, partly to make her feel better, but mostly so she and June would leave.

"I hope so," said May. She shrugged. "A

lot of girls are trying out. I don't know what's going to happen."

"I know the feeling," I told her. Even though the last few days with Leo were a welcome distraction, there was so much drama over what happened New Year's Eve. I have this gnawing feeling there's more to come. May said it perfectly.

I don't know what's going to happen.

Sometimes doing something is worse than doing nothing.

—*Meredith Grey*

Last night after May left my room, she came back. She wanted to know if she could sleep with me. I felt bad so I let her, but she kept tossing and turning and sticking her knees and elbows into me. She finally fell asleep, but I couldn't. My brain was racing.

I hadn't expected Brynn to show up at the diner and confront anyone. She definitely hasn't been acting like the Brynn I used to know and love. Plus, now Emily and Vanessa have been drawn into what's going on, so I don't know what to expect at dance. They're clearly Team Brynn.

I was also thinking about what's going to happen with Sophie and Billy. They kissed. As Leo said, that's between them. In theory, it doesn't affect me. But the reality is they're my best friends. If they start going out, will they spend all their time together? Without me?

And there's Leo. We're definitely more than friends, but we're not boyfriend and girlfriend. It's not that I necessarily want to go out with him. I like the way things are now, but I have no idea what it will be like when I'm here and he's off at school. I just Googled long distance relationships where you're more than friends but not going out. It's not even a category.

Argh.

After all this reflection and Googling, I'm not any wiser. But I am late for school.

6:44 p.m.
Mad

I had a bad feeling Brynn was going to lash out, but I seriously underestimated what she would do. Ms. Baumann had given us winter break off, so today was our first day back at practice since the confrontation at the New Year's Day brunch.

At break, Emily came up to me and said Brynn told her I was happy when Emily sprained her ankle last semester and I got to dance her solo in the show. "Is that true?" she asked.

"That's crazy," I said.

But Emily didn't seem convinced. "It kind of makes sense that you'd be happy you got to take my place."

"I can't believe you'd think I'd be happy you hurt yourself," I told her.

Emily eyed me accusatorily. "Brynn said that would be your reaction."

"Of course, that's my reaction. What other reaction is there?" But Emily didn't answer. I don't know if I made my point or not.

It's so dumb. Part of me doesn't care.

Wednesday, January 7, 10:02 p.m.
Furious

I could have gotten over what Brynn told
Emily. It was absurd. Plus, I have a hard time
thinking that Emily really believes it's true.

I also could have gotten over the fact that
yesterday Vanessa came up to me after dance
and said that she's really sad for Brynn that I
wasn't there for her when she was obviously
going through a hard time, and that it just
makes her wonder how committed I am to
being part of the dance team. Seriously?

But now I'm truly mad.

I just found out Brynn is having a spa day at
her house on Saturday afternoon and invited
all the freshman girls on the dance team . . .
EXCEPT ME!

When Kate Walls texted me saying how
much fun it's going to be that we'll all be
together at Brynn's for manis and pedis, I felt
like I was going to throw up. I don't want to be
excluded from something all the ninth graders on
the team are doing. My first reaction was to call
Brynn and say something, but what's the point?

Even if she had invited me, the last place I want to be is with her.

Thursday, January 8, 10:17 p.m.
Annoyed

Leo texted me when he got to school, but tonight was our first live conversation since he left for college. He was so upbeat about his classes and the unlimited cereal bar in the morning and the fact that his dorm is only 163 to 165 steps from the library. He said he counted twice and got a slightly different number both times and that by his estimation some dorms are more than 600 steps from the library.

Then he asked me what's going on with me. I started to tell him about the girl drama going on in dance, but I stopped myself. It seemed trivial in comparison, and it was a little unsettling that a.) I don't even want to talk about my own life, and b.) Leo has only been gone four days, and I already feel like there's stuff I can't tell him.

Then I heard talking and laughter in the

background, and Leo said he had to go because he had a floor meeting and it was starting. I don't even know what a floor meeting is, but I know it includes other people because I heard them. I pictured Leo surrounded by those people. College people.

Annoying.

Saturday, January 10, 4:10 p.m.
Surprised (not in a good way)

Today was the day the dance team went to Brynn's house.

I told Sophie what they were doing without me, and she suggested we have our own spa day, so I went over to Gaga's, and we sat on the floor of Sophie's room and painted our fingernails and toenails.

While we were waiting for them to dry, I noticed something I didn't remember seeing the last time I was there— a bright-colored, carved wooden fish on her bookshelf. "Is that new?" I asked motioning to the fish.

Sophie smiled. She got up and got the fish from the bookshelf and brought it over so I could get a better look. "Billy brought it back to me from his trip to Mexico. Cool, huh?"

I told her I thought it was, but what I was really thinking was that if Billy brought Sophie a gift back from Mexico, he must like her. I already had a feeling he did, especially when I saw them kiss on New Year's Eve. But Billy was in Mexico over Christmas, which means he got her the fish before they kissed. It was proof that Sophie and Billy are going to get together.

It used to be an *if*. Now it's a *when*.

I don't know why that surprised me. Or upset me. But as I waited for my toes to dry, I pictured Sophie and Billy as a couple, Brynn with the dance team, and Leo off with a bunch of college people. Then I pictured myself. Alone. I felt stupid for picturing myself like that. Sophie and I were supposed to be having a spa day.

Not a pity party.

Hold fast to dreams

For if dreams die

Life is a broken-winged bird

That cannot fly.

—*Langston Hughes*, Dreams

Monday, January 12, 5:59 p.m.
Home from dance

Things aren't better with Brynn, not that I thought they would be. But I hadn't anticipated that she would use her spa day on Saturday to try to turn all the other freshman on the dance against me.

I think it's a pretty safe assumption that she told them why she hadn't invited me, based on the fact that no one seemed to want anything to do with me at practice. I was ostracized like Hester Prynne in *The Scarlet Letter* (which we're reading in English.) And as I was leaving practice, Kate came up to me and said she was sorry she mentioned the spa day to me. "I felt bad," she said. "I didn't realize you and Brynn aren't friends anymore."

"No problem," I said.

Then Kate said "Brynn told everyone what Sophie did at the party." She made a face like just the memory of what Brynn told her was unpleasant. "I didn't see it. But it sounded bad—Sophie moving in on Billy like that. It sounds like she was being pretty aggressive." She raised a brow like she was waiting for me to respond.

I felt like I had to defend Sophie, even though I really didn't want to get dragged into this. "Since you didn't see it, don't you think you're being pretty judgmental?"

Kate ignored my question. "I know she's related to you or something, but it's wrong that she kissed someone else's boyfriend."

"Billy isn't Brynn's boyfriend anymore."

Kate looked at me like she couldn't believe I'd said that. "Is. Was. Same difference. And you're supposed to be her best friend."

"*Was.* I was her best friend," I said.

Kate looked at me like she couldn't believe those words had come out of my mouth. "Brynn said you don't get it, and it's a shame," Kate said.

I couldn't believe she was getting so involved in something that clearly had nothing to do with her. A lot happened between Brynn and me, and Brynn had clearly only told her half of the story. I thought about telling Kate my side of things, but what was the point? She was just one person on the team. There were lots of others. What was I supposed to do? Go person to person and repeat myself? Plus, Kate had already picked her side. I slung my backpack over my shoulder and left.

I'd heard enough for one day.

Tuesday, January 13
Study Hall

As Sophie and I were leaving lunch, she told me that Beth Schimberg told her that Kelly Blake said she heard the reason Brynn and I aren't friends anymore is because she (Sophie) likes Billy, and I (April) didn't do anything to stop it.

"Isn't that nuts?" said Sophie. "I mean seriously, who thinks like that?"

I hadn't told Sophie what was happening on the dance team, because I knew it would make her feel awful if she thought people were being mean to me because of something she did. Plus, it seemed like the problem was pretty contained to just the girls on the dance team. But if Brynn was starting to drag in other random people like Beth and Kelly, who were now bringing Sophie into the drama, I didn't have much of a choice.

"I guess Brynn can be pretty vindictive when she's upset," I said to Sophie.

"But to say that the two of you aren't friends because I like Billy is ridiculous." Sophie paused, and then looked at me. "I'm going to try to talk to her," she said.

I shook my head. "I don't think you should get into it with Brynn," I said. "I've known her for a long time and I promise, there's nothing you can say that could make matters better."

"They can't get worse," said Sophie.

Unfortunately, I think they can.

9:45 p.m.
Just talked to Sophie
Who talked to Billy
About Brynn

Sophie called me tonight right when I'd
gotten out of the shower. I was still soaking wet
and wasn't even going to answer, but I dried off
my hand and one side of my head and face so I
could talk.

"I told Billy what Brynn has been saying
about you, and Billy told me that he's going
to try to talk to Brynn," said Sophie as soon as
I answered the phone. "He thinks the issue is
between Brynn and him."

"That's good," I said. But then I told Sophie
I had to go. I didn't want to hear anymore
about what Sophie told Billy or what Billy was
planning to say to Brynn. It was late. I was
wet. And I'd spent way too much time today
on this topic.

Here's a little piece of good news: I fixed my problems, at least the ones with the dance team.

There has been so much tension all week. Everyone knows Brynn and I aren't friends anymore, and they've all been acting like they had to choose sides. Brynn pretty much had everyone convinced they needed to choose her side, which sucked for me personally, but also has been affecting the group dance the freshman girls have been working on for our next competition.

And I wasn't the only one who thought so. When Ms. Baumann criticized our group and told us our timing was off, I knew it was time to act. I appealed to Emily's sense of teamwork. "Whatever problems exist between Brynn and me shouldn't affect the team," I said at break today. "We need to all work together if we want to do well."

Emily, who loves dance even more than drama (which she clearly likes a lot), seemed relieved. "I think so too," she said. When break was over, she made a speech to our group about how we all need to work together. Everyone agreed to do their part, even Brynn. When we started dancing, she avoided dancing near me or looking in my direction, which made things kind of awkward.

But hey . . . I'll take awkward over ostracized.

9:17 p.m.
Feeling pretty good

I felt pretty good about what happened in dance, so I decided to call Leo (who I haven't spoken to in a week) and tell him about it. But when I called, he didn't pick up. I hope he'll call back.

11:17 p.m.
Going to sleep

He didn't.

Friday, January 16, 8:13 p.m.

Text from Leo

Leo: Sorry I didn't call you back last night.

Leo: First college test today. I had to study.

Me: No problem!

Me: Hope it went well.

Leo: Me too. Hard to tell.

Leo: I'll call you this weekend.

Me: 🙂

Leo: Is that a smiley face?

Me: Yes.

Leo: 🙂 🙂 🙂

Me: 🙂

Saturday, January 16, 10:35 p.m.

Leo didn't call today. That makes it sound like I sat around all day waiting for him to, which I didn't. I did a lot of things (while I was waiting for him to call), including calling Sophie to see if she wanted to do something. She said she was doing something with Billy. She hesitated, then said I could come along too if I wanted. But the way she said it made me feel like she only invited me because she felt like she had to.

Maybe I was imagining things. Maybe I wasn't.

But I didn't go.

Sunday, January 17, 10:02 p.m.
Going to bed

Leo didn't call today either.

But that's OK because I would have been too busy to take his call. When I woke up, I made a decision to have a positive, productive day versus a day spent ruminating (vocab word) on the fact that Leo hasn't called back or that Sophie and Billy did something together yesterday and didn't really (at least, in my opinion) want me to come along or that my lifelong (former) best friend has turned into an out-of-control, manipulative stranger.

First, I cleaned out my backpack and went for a run. For breakfast I had waffles, bacon, and orange slices and savored (another vocab word) every bite. Then I helped Dad clean out the garage.

When we were done, I showered, did my Bio homework, and then watched seven episodes of *SpongeBob* with May and June. That's the second-highest number of consecutive episodes I've watched of a show I don't like. Since I was consciously being positive, I made a lot of upbeat comments while I was watching it like, "Isn't that stupid sponge funny?" Then I made a scrunched up weird face and told May and June I was trying to imitate SpongeBob.

May and June found my imitation to be hysterical. They were literally on the floor, laughing. Even Mom commented about how sweet it was to see us laughing and having fun together.

It might seem no human could shove any more positive, productive things into a day, but I did. When we finished watching TV, I asked my sisters if either of them needed any help with their homework. June said she did, so I quizzed her on her spelling words, even though I knew she knew them cold before we'd started.

"Can you believe how fast I learned those?" June asked when we'd gone through the list.

"You're a cracker-jack speller," I said.

"What does that mean?" she asked. I told her she should look it up, and then (because I momentarily had forgotten, but quickly remembered that I was being positive), I said she could use my computer to do so. If that's not the face of positivity, I don't know what is. Oh, by the way, Leo did not call today.

Oops! Did that sound negative?

11:17 p.m.
Can't sleep

I think today's positivity is keeping me awake. So I'm going to say what's really on my mind, and it's not very positive: there's way too much drama in my life and I'm sick of it.

I'm sick of Leo saying he's going to call and not doing it.

I'm sick of wondering what's going to happen between Billy and Sophie. I think I already know what's going to happen. But I don't like wondering when they ask me to do something if they're asking because they want to or because they feel like they have to.

And I'm really sick of thinking about Brynn and wondering what's going to happen. Will we ever speak again? Will we be enemies throughout high school, and then sometime down the road, like at graduation, finally talk about it, realize it was silly, and make up? Or will it be one of those things where we bump into each other years from now as adults, and say something really lame like, "Hey, I remember you. Didn't we used to be friends?"

There you have it.

The girl formerly known as Miss Positivity, is going to sleep.

Just because I don't care doesn't mean I don't understand.

—*Homer Simpson*

Leo: Sorry didn't call this weekend.

Leo: I had a lot of studying to do.

Me: A test?

Leo: Two of them this week.

Me: Good luck.

Leo: Thanks

I waited. I thought Leo would write more. I even turned my phone off and on again in case he'd written more and there was some technical glitch with the phone that prevented texts from coming through. But nothing came through, which makes me think I have a problem. I'm just not sure if it's a phone problem or a Leo problem.

Actually, I'm pretty sure.

Tuesday, January 20, 6:17 p.m.
Talked to Sophie

Sophie just called and told me that she was in the bathroom after school today and overheard Kelly Blake and Julia Lozano talking about her. "What did they say?" I asked.

"Kelly told Julia that Brynn told her Billy called her and said I kissed him at the party on New Year's Eve, and that he was shocked when it happened and didn't know what to do. Then she said Brynn said he told her he doesn't like me but he doesn't want to hurt my feelings and that he's hoping it just dies out."

It made me mad at Brynn all over again. I don't know exactly what Billy said when he called her, but I know it wasn't that. "You know Billy didn't say any of that, right?"

Sophie hesitated for a beat too long. I could tell she wasn't sure. "I hope he didn't say it."

"Of course he didn't," I said. I knew in her rational mind she had to know that. "Did you say anything to Kelly and Julia?" I asked.

"I was using the bathroom," said Sophie. "But anyway, I don't care what other people have to say."

She might not, but I do.

Wednesday, January 21, 6:45 p.m.
Confronted Brynn

Today at dance, Brynn and I ended up next to each other when Ms. Baumann rearranged our dance formation. When I accidentally bumped into her (which I'd been careful not to do but couldn't help doing when Kate tripped and almost knocked me down), Brynn groaned loudly. The girls in the row in front of us turned around to see what had happened.

I'd had enough, plus I wanted to say something to her about what Sophie told me.

At break, I followed her into the bathroom. When she came out of her stall, I said, "I heard what you're telling people about Sophie. Don't spread lies about her."

"Are you threatening me?" she asked.

"That's ridiculous," I said to Brynn. It was just the two of us in the bathroom. It seemed like the perfect moment to say what was really on my mind. "This whole thing has gotten out of hand. I'm sorry you're hurt, but we should try to get past this."

I was offering Brynn an olive branch, but she looked at me like I was asking her to poison her dog. "Do you have any idea what it feels like to be me?" she asked.

I couldn't believe that was her response when I'd tried so hard to be nice. I was officially done. "No," I said. "I don't."

Fortunately.

Thursday, January 22, 7:02 p.m.
Home from dance practice
Exhausted

Even though things with the freshman girls on the team aren't as strained as they were a couple weeks ago, it's exhausting being on the same team and in the same dance with Brynn while we're not talking to each other. We've developed an elaborate system for avoiding each other.

When we're in formation for the dance, her position is all the way to the front left, and I'm in the back right. If Ms. Baumann is talking to us and we're gathered around her huddle-style, Brynn and I avoid all eye and body contact. And at break, she goes to the bathroom first while I get a drink of water, then when she comes out, I go in.

It takes effort, but I guess you could say it works.

Tuesday, January 27, 9:17 p.m.
SGA calls
Billy and Sophie answer

SGA at Faraway High School must be busier than the CIA, FBI and all other three-letter government agencies because every time I see Sophie and Billy, they're always coming from or going to a meeting, and they're always laughing and smiling.

Does that bother me? It shouldn't.

But sometimes it does.

Friday, January 30, 6:17 p.m.
Leo called

Leo finally called and apologized for not having called. "I know it's been a while. College is a lot more work than I'm used to," he said. He talked for a long time about tests and labs and papers he's been working on.

I wasn't feeling forgiving. I had cramps and I'd been in a bad mood for a few days. Not that it was all related to Leo, but he was in the wrong place at the wrong time. "Even if you're busy, it seems like you'd have time for a quick call once in a while." My voice had an edge.

"I'm sorry," said Leo.

He was quiet. It seemed like he was waiting for me to say, *I forgive you*, but I didn't. "April, what's going on?" he asked.

I realized I wanted to get things off my chest, but it wasn't easy to say what I was thinking. "Um, I guess . . . I feel like I care more about our friendship than you do."

"That's not true," said Leo.

"It seems like it is," I said a little more boldly.

Leo hesitated. "It's not that. I promise."

"Then what is it?" I asked. I wanted to know.

I heard someone talking in the background. It was a girl's voice. "Hold on," said Leo.

"I'm coming," I heard him say. But he wasn't talking to me.

"I have to go now. I'm going to dinner with my roommate and another friend. But I'll be home in two weeks, and we'll talk more." His voice was matter-of-fact, like I'd asked for his notes from chemistry classes and he could just fill me in whenever we had more time.

Hmm, chemistry. I wonder if we have any?

9:45 p.m.

I keep thinking about my conversation with Leo.

I can't imagine what *it* is and why he couldn't or wouldn't tell me over the phone. Maybe he has a girlfriend and he doesn't want to tell me about her over the phone. Maybe that's who he was going to dinner with.

I've been thinking about it all night and it seems like that's the only thing it could be. I'm going to ask him about it next time he calls.

If there's a next time.

Saturday, January 31, 2:45 p.m.
At Flora's Fashions with Mom

I went to the store with Mom this morning. Another department store placed an order, so she had a lot to do and I volunteered to help out. The morning was really busy. There were a lot of customers coming in and out, so while Mom helped them, I answered the phone and put clothes that people tried on back on the racks.

When the morning rush died down, I went next door to the deli to get sandwiches for us. As I watched the new guy make my sandwiches, I smiled to myself as I pictured Leo making sandwiches in his dorm room. Then I stopped smiling when I thought about the possibility of him making them for his girlfriend too.

When I went back to the store with the

sandwiches, Mom hung her *back in an hour* sign on the door, and we sat down to eat. "What's the matter?" she asked. "You look upset."

"Nothing," I lied. I didn't want to get into it with her. I pointed to the bolts of crimson, white, and teal fabrics stacked neatly behind the counter. "Are those for the new order?" I asked.

That was a subject Mom was happy to talk about. She got up and went to the counter. When she came back she had a large notebook. "These are the designs," she said as she showed me pages filled with skirts, tops, and pants.

"They look great!" I said to Mom.

"Thanks, honey." She smiled like she really did appreciate my stamp of approval. "I'm pleased with how well everything is going. It's a dream come true, really."

Talking about Mom's hopes and dreams was a welcome distraction from everything I'd been thinking about lately. "How did you know what you wanted to be?"

Mom took a long sip from her water bottle before she answered. "When I was a little girl,

I used to spend hours at the sewing machine. I've always wanted to be a fashion designer, even when I was your age."

As I ate my sandwich, I tried to picture my life. It wasn't hard to do. I saw myself tangled up in all the drama that's been swirling around me for a while now. I can't say I liked what I saw.

You can be the moon and still be jealous of the stars.

—Gary Allan

Thursday, February 5, 10:42 p.m.
May just left my room

"Shouldn't you be asleep?" I asked May when she came into my room. It was a school night and was way past her bedtime.

"I can't fall asleep," she said.

I could tell with one look there was a problem. "What happened?"

May sat down on the edge of my bed. "I made the middle school softball team."

"I know." We'd already celebrated her accomplishment at dinner tonight. "So what's the problem?" I was starting to lose patience.

I watched as May picked at a scab on her ankle. "The problem is that Krystal Connery is on the team too, and after Coach Newman announced the sixth graders who made the team, Krystal came over to me and said I really do look like a boy. She asked some of the other girls to raise their hands if they thought so too." May paused. "I think I should grow out my hair."

I let out an exasperated breath. "May, I thought you weren't having any more problems with Krystal." It was a question, not a statement.

"I wasn't." May shrugged. "Until now."

I scooted down to the end of the bed and looked at May. "You don't need to grow out your hair if you like it the way it is. It looks cute short." Then I looped an arm around her. "Don't worry," I said. "We're going to take care of this problem."

Once and for all.

Saturday, February 6, 4:45 p.m.
Post-dance competition
Post-home visit to Krystal

When I got home from the dance
competition today, I didn't even bother to
change out of my leotard and tights. I threw
on some jeans and a sweater and grabbed my
jacket. "Let's go," I said to May. We walked
together to Krystal's house. When we got
there, I rang the bell.

"You're not going to do anything crazy, are
you?" May asked as we waited for someone
to answer.

"Like what?" I'd told her on the way
over that all I was going to do was talk to
Krystal. I don't know what May was thinking,
but it was easy to see her imagination was
working overtime.

May visibly stiffened when Krystal's mom
answered the door. "Aren't you May? The
young star on Krystal's soccer team?" she asked.

May shrugged like she was too modest
to answer that question. I could tell she was
uncomfortable and unsure where Krystal's

mom was going with that, but Krystal's mom was sweet. "Well, I recognize you from the games. Faraway Middle is lucky to have you. Hold on," she said with a smile. "I'll get Krystal."

"See, so far so good," I said to May. She kicked me in the shin to be quiet.

"Watch it!" I said. "I'm not a soccer ball."

May smiled at my attempt at humor, but her smile vanished as soon as Krystal opened the door. "What are you doing here?" she asked looking at me.

I made a mental note that apples actually can fall far from the tree. Krystal clearly had none of her mother's warmth. "I came to talk to you," I said to Krystal.

She started to close the door like she wasn't interested in hearing what I had to say, but her mother came up behind her before she could shut us out. "Invite your friends inside. I'll put out some cookies."

"That sounds great!" I said to Krystal's mom. Krystal rolled her eyes as we all followed her mom to the kitchen. She knew she didn't have a choice.

May, Krystal, and I sat down. "I'll leave you girls alone," said Mrs. Connery after she put a plate of oatmeal raisin cookies and a pitcher of lemonade on the table.

I took a cookie from the plate and took a bite. "Mmm," I said.

Krystal looked at me like she didn't care what I thought of the cookie.

I cleared my throat. "I brought May here today because I think the time has come for the two of you to be friends."

Krystal and May both looked at me like they were shocked that's what I'd said. "You're the two best athletes at the middle school. You have a lot of years of sports ahead of you, and it will be good for your teams if you get along."

Krystal didn't respond, and neither did May. I kept going. "Krystal, you're an incredible athlete and everyone knows it. You're amazing at whatever sport you play. Before May got to the middle school, you had to carry whatever team you were on by yourself. Now you and

May are both great in your positions. Think how much better your teams can be if you work together."

Krystal didn't respond. I could see she was taking in what I'd said. I didn't want to get too philosophical on her, but I knew it was now or never. "Jealousy is an ugly emotion. It exposes your fears. It will ruin your life."

May looked like she was going to throw up and Krystal looked doubtful. "Isn't that a little dramatic?" she asked.

I had to give her that. "Maybe, but trust me when I tell you jealousy can mess things up in a big way."

"How do you know?" asked Krystal.

I thought about telling her what happened with Brynn when she got jealous about Billy and Sophie's relationship, but it was TMI and beside the point. "It happened to a friend of mine."

I looked at Krystal and waited. I'd said enough, so the next move was hers. But to my surprise, May spoke up. "Krystal, you're a great athlete. It's awesome having someone so good on the soccer team. I think we have a strong softball team too." May shrugged. "I'm glad I get to play with you."

Krystal smiled and looked pleasantly surprised. She hesitated. "You too, May. Teammates?" she said.

"Teammates," said May.

Krystal grinned and so did May. I had a mouth full of cookie, so it was a little hard for me to, but as soon as I washed my cookie down with some lemonade, I high-fived them both. Then I told May it was time to go.

In the big sister department, I'd done enough good for one day.

6:25 p.m.
Disappointed

I just called Leo. I wanted to tell him what happened with May, but I got his voicemail.

I left a message. Maybe he'll call back.

Or maybe he won't.

10:49 p.m.

~~Asleep~~

Awake

Leo called back, but I was actually already asleep. "What's up?" he said into the phone. I did my best to shake myself awake, but as I started telling him what happened with May and Krystal, I heard laughter in the background. I finished the story, but when I did all Leo said was, "That's great."

I guess that's how most people would respond. From most people, that would be fine. But Leo always has something witty, unique, or insightful to say.

So hearing him say, *"That's great"* . . . just wasn't so great.

*Most folks are as happy as they
make up their minds to be.*

—Abraham Lincoln

Tuesday, February 10, 7:09 p.m.
Billy's big news

Since we'd worked so hard to prepare for
the competition on Saturday and don't have
another one coming up for over a month, Ms.
Baumann gave us the week off of practice.
Yesterday, it felt weird leaving school and going
home at 3:15, so this morning I asked Billy if
he wanted to hang out after school.

We went to his house, and it was a lot like
old times. His mom gave me a big hug when
I got there and said how happy she was to see

me. Billy and I ate popcorn and mini Reese's, and drank lemonade at his kitchen table. Then we hung out in his room, looking at old photos and listening to music. That was our pattern for as long as I can remember. The only thing that was different this time was that it didn't include Brynn.

Since third grade, it had been the three of us. We did everything together, even over the summers. I have so many memories of my arms linked through theirs as we walked the path from the Arts and Crafts shop or the tennis courts back to our bunks at camp. We were the Three Musketeers for a long time.

I took a box of old photos of us from grade school from a shelf over Billy's desk and settled into the floor of his room next to him. "It's kind of weird without her," I said. Billy knew who I meant.

"Yeah," he said. But he didn't make a move to look through the photos. I wasn't sure he felt as nostalgic as he sounded.

"Do you miss being friends with her?" I asked.

Billy let out a sigh. "I've tried talking to her," he said. "I even went over to her house on New Year's Day after the confrontation at the diner. I wanted her to know I was really sorry about what happened between us. But her mom came to the door and said Brynn didn't want to talk to me."

"Was Mrs. Stephens mad?" I asked. I'd wondered what Brynn's mom knows about why Billy broke up with her or how our friendship fell apart. Whatever she knows, it's only from Brynn's perspective, and I'm just not sure she has any idea how overly dramatic and frustrating Brynn can be.

"Mrs. Stephens is always nice, so it was hard to tell," said Billy. "I told her to tell Brynn that I'm sorry about everything. I think she understood." He shrugged, then kept talking. "I miss the way we used to be. You know, the Three Musketeers. But it hasn't been that way for a while."

I stood up and put the box of photos back on the shelf. Billy was right. A lot changed when he and I started going out at the end of the summer before eighth grade. It got even more complicated when he and Brynn started going out this past summer.

When I sat back down, Billy exhaled. "I've done everything I can," he said, like he was through trying to make things better with Brynn.

"I get it," I said to Billy. "I've tried to talk to Brynn too. There are lots of things I'd still like to say to her. But she's made it clear she doesn't want anything to do with me."

When I finished talking, Billy cleared his throat. "April, I'm going to ask Sophie out." His words sat between us for a second, and I could tell he was waiting for my response.

"Finally!" I said.

We both laughed. Billy was relieved, and in a way, I was too. I waited to see if he was going to give me details. How. When. Where. But he didn't, and I didn't feel like I could ask. Even though we're friends again, we used to go out, so it just felt weird to ask him how he was going to ask out another girl.

"Want to listen to some music?" I asked Billy.

He grinned. "You know I do."

Some things will never change. Billy will always love listening to music. As we sat side by side listening, I felt happy for Billy.

It's a little weird that he went out with me, then Brynn, and now Sophie. I guess weirder things have happened. (I'm not sure what.) But he and Sophie seem to fit. And best of all, the truth will be out and hopefully everyone can move on.

Including Brynn.

Wednesday, February 11, 5:44 p.m.
Sophie is a rule-breaker (in a good way)

Today in Bio, Sophie asked me if I would go with her after school to the Cold Shack. "I have something important to tell you," she said.

I tried to get out of her what it was about, but she wouldn't say. I thought it might have something to do with her parents. Valentine's Day is Saturday, and I had a feeling she was thinking they're going to get back together or something, but Sophie said she wasn't saying a word until we were settled into our favorite booth with a scoop each of our new favorite flavor, Mocha Chip.

By the time we got our ice cream, I couldn't wait a second longer to hear her news. "Spill it," I said.

Sophie took a bite of ice cream. "Mmm, delicious!" She was enjoying this way too much.

"Out with it!"

"Patience is a virtue," said Sophie. She took another bite. And another.

"C'mon!" I said. "You have to tell me now."

Sophie smiled and pushed her cup aside. "OK," she said. "What I wanted to tell you is that I'm going to ask Billy out. On Valentine's Day."

Even though it's hard to choke on ice cream, I'm pretty sure I did. "Like out on a date?" I asked, though I was pretty sure that wasn't what she meant.

"No, silly, I'm going to ask Billy if he wants to be my boyfriend."

Part of me wanted to tell her Billy was already planning to ask her out. But I knew I couldn't betray his confidence. And I didn't want to spoil it for her.

"Sophie, you know Faraway is pretty old-fashioned, right? Usually, the boy asks the girl out, not the other way around."

Sophie shook her head at my explanation. "That's ridiculous."

"I agree," I said. "But I don't make the rules."

"Well I don't care who makes them. I like Billy, and I'm going to ask him out on Valentine's Day." She was actually blushing. "I thought about different ways of doing it. But everything I thought of seemed like it belonged in a bad movie. I'm just going to go to his house, ring his doorbell, and ask him if he wants to go out."

As Sophie talked, it was easy to see how much she likes Billy. And I know he likes her. I don't think it matters who asks who out.

Something tells me they're going to be happy together.

9:17 p.m.
Just hung up with Leo

Leo called to say he'll be home for the weekend on Friday, and we made a plan to meet in the park. "I can't wait to see you," he said.

I wanted to say something light or clever in response. Even something simple like, "Me too!" But those words wouldn't come out. So many times when I'd called him, he couldn't talk or didn't return my call for days. It was confusing to hear him say he's excited to see me. I wasn't sure what to say to him, so I went with the truth. "Leo, we have stuff to talk about."

Leo laughed. "April, we always have stuff to talk about." I couldn't tell if he was being straightforward or sarcastic.

I guess I have to wait until Friday to find out.

Life moves pretty fast. If you don't

stop and look around once in a while,

you could miss it.

—*Ferris Bueller*

Friday, February 13, 6:55 p.m.
Home from the park

I'd been worried about meeting Leo in the park since we'd talked the other day. I had an idea of what I wanted to say to him. I'd even rehearsed it in my head on the way to the park. I just wasn't confident it would come out the way I wanted it to. Plus, it was Friday the 13th, which I took as a bad sign. Good things never happen on Friday the 13th.

But as I walked toward the slide on the playground where we'd agreed to meet, Leo smiled and waved me over, and my anxiety melted into excitement.

"April Elizabeth Sinclair, in person!" he said and gave me a hug.

I smiled. Leo's hair was longer, and he looked cuter than I'd remembered. Plus I couldn't believe he remembered my middle name. I was pretty sure I'd only told it to him once.

He tapped the side of his head, like he'd read my mind. "It's a little embarrassing to admit this, but I've got a knack for remembering all the little things you tell me." He motioned to a nearby bench and we sat down.

"Hmm," I said flirtatiously. "Is that a sign of liking someone?"

Leo raised a brow at me like the answer to my question was obvious. But it wasn't. At least not to me.

"Leo," I said tentatively.

"Henry," he said. "If you're wondering, my middle name is Henry. I've always thought it's a handsome name, in a British sort of way." He cleared his throat. "Leo Henry," he said with a British accent.

I laughed. It was so silly and so him.

He kept talking. "As I'm sure you know, Elizabeth is also a British name. I like that we both have British middle names. It's just one of the things we have in common." Leo looked at me like he was gauging my reaction.

There might be some things we have in common, but we also have some pretty big differences, like the fact that I'm still in high school, and now, he's a college student. And possibly, a college student with a girlfriend.

"Leo, we need to talk." I launched into the speech I'd rehearsed on the way to the park. "Since you went to college . . . you say you're going to call, then you don't. I try to tell you things, and you don't really respond." I paused. "I'm sure college is a lot of work, but I think there's more to it."

"You're right," said Leo. "There is."

I waited for him to say what I was pretty sure was coming next.

But he surprised me. "I didn't like going to high school because I didn't fit in," Leo said. "I thought college would be better."

His face crinkled like he was having a hard time saying what came next. "But I'm still two years younger than everyone else there. To be honest, I'm not really making many friends."

"That's it?" I asked.

Leo looked confused. "That's it," he said sarcastically.

I couldn't help it, but I started laughing.

Leo looked mad. "How's that funny?" he asked.

"I'm sorry," I said between giggles. "I'm not laughing at you. I'm laughing because I'm relieved. I thought you were going to tell me you have a girlfriend."

"A girlfriend?" Leo looked shocked.

"Yeah, I thought the reason you didn't have time to talk to me was because you were spending your time talking to someone else."

Leo shook his head like I couldn't have been any further off.

Even though part of me was relieved, I felt bad for Leo that he was having a hard time making friends. I did my best to put on a serious face. "Maybe it just takes time to make new friends," I said.

"Yeah," said Leo. But he didn't sound convinced.

I hadn't realized what a big adjustment college would be. I felt kind of silly about the rest of what I'd planned to say to Leo.

He looked at me. "What? I know you're thinking something but not saying it." He poked me lightly in the ribs.

"Well," I said taking a deep breath. "I was going to say that so much has changed since you left. You're in college, with this whole other life." I shrugged. "I don't know. I feel like we should break up."

The corners of Leo's eyes turned up, like he was trying to hold back a smile. "April, how are we supposed to break up if we're not even going out?"

I could feel my face turning red.

Leo apologized. "I wasn't making fun of you, just a point. I guess that's the scientist in me." He paused. "I know what you mean," he said. "We're in different places. We should focus on what we're each doing. . . . But it doesn't mean we can't be friends."

I exhaled. I want to stay friends with Leo, and it was such a relief to know he does too, even if there are challenges.

Leo kept talking. "I think what you're saying is that we need an un-breakup."

I raised a brow at him. "What's your definition of an un-breakup?" I couldn't wait to hear.

Leo straightened his glasses. "Since we're technically not going out, we can't technically break up. However, I would say what we've been doing is un-going out, which I define as feeling like you're going out with someone without actually doing it."

I laughed. "That's exactly how I feel," I said to Leo.

"Right," said Leo, continuing on like it was validating to know we were on the same page. "As much as I've enjoyed un-going out with you, I agree it's in both our best interests to un-break up."

I tucked a stray hair behind my ear. This

had been too easy and almost pleasant. "So it's official? We're un-broken up?" I asked, smiling.

Leo looked at me like he was choosing his words carefully. "Not so fast," he said. "We're officially un-broken up. But I really like talking to you, April. I hope that when either of us has something to say, we pick up the phone and make a call." Leo paused. "I guess what I'm saying is that I'd like to be friends who talk."

"I'd like that a lot," I said to Leo.

He smiled. "Well in honor of being officially un-broken up and friends who talk, I have a present for you."

I laughed. Leo is clearly a genius, but sometimes he can be so nonsensical. "Why would you give me a present when we're un-breaking up?" I asked.

Leo was laughing too. "Because I bought it before I knew that's what we would be doing. And I think you'll like it just the same if we're un-going out or un-broken up."

Then he reached behind the bench for a bag. "I actually have a few presents for you," he said. Leo took a University of Alabama baseball cap out of the bag and put it on my head. "Crimson is your color," he said. Then he pulled out the biggest box of Valentine's candy I'd ever seen. "For you," he said.

"Wow! It's huge!"

"It was on sale in the book store," said Leo. "So if the candy tastes like it was from last year, you'll know why."

I laughed. Then I got serious. "Leo, I feel bad. I didn't get you a present."

Leo shrugged. "I'm just glad to see you again." His face reddened when he said it. He sounded so sweet and sincere.

I thought about what Mom has said about us figuring it out. I couldn't imagine not being friends with Leo. I reached up and hugged him hard, and then I looked across the park. "Want to swing?" I asked.

Leo nodded that he did. So we swung, and we slid, and then we climbed to the top of the monkey bars. We probably looked like little kids on a play date, but I didn't care. It was the most fun I'd had on a playground in a long time.

Then Leo walked me home. I'll admit I felt a little sad. It wasn't the end of something, like what happened with Brynn. But still, I knew things would be different from now on.

Leo and I said good-bye, and as I walked inside with my hat on my head and my candy tucked under my arm, I couldn't help but think that the day had been bittersweet.

8:59 p.m.
It's official

Sophie just called to tell me that Billy beat her to the punch. "We're going out!" she screamed into the phone.

"That's amazing!" I screamed back. All the times I've called her with good news, she's always been so excited for me. I wanted her to feel my enthusiasm.

"He said he wanted to do it the day before Valentine's Day, because he thought it would be unexpected, offbeat, and cool, like me." I could tell how much she loved his reasoning.

"I'm really happy for you," I told her. And I was.

But as Sophie chatted on about how Billy asked her out, I was thinking about what it will be like now that they're going out. They're my two best friends, and I hope that doesn't change.

"You still there?" asked Sophie.

I hadn't realized that I'd spaced out. "Sorry," I said.

"What's up?" asked Sophie.

I didn't want to lie. "I'm just worried we'll never do stuff together now," I said honestly.

"I'd never be that kind of friend," said Sophie.

She sounded so definite, I had to believe her. But everything got so complicated when Brynn and Billy started going out. It's just kind of hard for me not to be worried now that Sophie and Billy are dating.

I guess only time will tell what their relationship will be like, and for that matter, how other people will react. Like Brynn. I know this will be hard for her. She really liked Billy. Part of me wishes I could be there for her. I know she'll need a friend. But I can't be her friend unless she's willing to be a friend too. A real friend, the kind that meets in the middle, and listens, and doesn't spread gossip and rumors about you. Maybe one day she'll be like that again.

But I'm not holding my breath.

9:24 p.m.
Talked to Mom

Mom was at the kitchen table working on some sketches. I hadn't planned to talk to her, but when I saw her alone, I sat down and asked her if she had a few minutes.

"Of course," she said.

"Sophie and Billy are going out," I said as soon as she looked up from her sketchbook. As the words sat between us, I wasn't even sure why I'd told Mom. I don't usually share stuff like that with her. Maybe it was because she's been so involved lately in everything that's gone on with Brynn.

Mom was quiet for a minute. I knew she was thinking through all the implications of the two of them going out. "Does Brynn know?" she asked.

"Not yet," I said.

"How do you think she'll take it?" Mom asked.

I shrugged. "Probably not well. She hasn't taken much well lately."

"I'm sorry," said Mom.

"Thanks, Mom." I know she's my mom, but I appreciated her loyalty. "Lately everything has been so tense. Not only with Brynn, but with Leo being away at college, and in a way, with Sophie and Billy pulling me into how they were getting together."

I looked down at a hole in the leg of my pajamas. "I guess I feel pretty good that I've moved on from all the drama with Brynn. I cleared the air with Leo. And I was honest with Sophie about the idea of Billy and her dating."

Mom reached over and squeezed my hand. "I'm proud of you, April. Figuring out how to be a true friend and true to yourself at the same time is a sign of growing up."

I rolled my eyes. It was such a mom thing to say. But I got what she meant. Maybe I'm growing up, or maybe talking to Mom just made me feel better.

But for now, my life feels drama-free, and I want to keep it that way.

10:32 p.m.
May and June just left my room

As I was getting into bed, May and June came into my room and climbed into bed with me. They didn't even ask if they could—they just did. Normally, I would have been annoyed, but I went with it.

June told us about the Valentine's Day party they had in her classroom today, since the actual holiday falls on a Saturday. Her enthusiasm was infectious as she told us about the Valentines she got and the heart-shaped cookies her teacher brought in.

"Do you get to have Valentine parties when you go to middle school and high school?" June asked May and me.

"Kind of," said May. "We got doughnuts in Science class, and we did a word find in English. Mr. Stanford gave out Valentine candy to everyone, no matter how many words they found."

May and June looked at me, waiting to hear what I did at school to celebrate. Instead, I reached under my bed and pulled out the box of candy Leo gave me. "Who wants chocolate?" I asked.

May and June both squealed with happiness. "Where did you get that?" asked May.

"A friend gave it to me," I said.

I pulled the wrapper off the box, and the three of us sat curled up in my bed eating candy. We'd pick out a chocolate and guess what was inside it, and then I'd turn it over and push my finger into the back to see if we were right. If it had a filling that one of us liked, we'd eat it. If not, I put back it back in the box, which meant that the ones with caramel, toffee, or nuts all got eaten, and the ones with coconut and fruit filling got left behind. We picked, guessed, poked, and ate until we were full.

It was a fun end to the day. Just me with my sisters, eating chocolates that were possibly old but still delicious in my bed. Nothing big. Nothing bad. Nothing dramatic.

I guess I was wrong. Good things do happen on Friday the 13th.

Ten Reasons My Life Is Mostly Miserable

1. My mom: Flora.

2. My dad: Rex.

3. My little sister: May.

4. My baby sister: June.

5. My dog: Gilligan.

6. My town: Faraway, Alabama.

7. My nose: too big.

8. My butt: too small.

9. My boobs: uneven.

10. My mouth. Especially when it is talking to cute boys.

THE MOSTLY MISERABLE LIFE OF APRIL SINCLAIR

About the Author

Laurie Friedman's favorite time of year while growing up was Thanksgiving through Valentine's Day. She loved celebrating holidays and remembers lots of fun times at holiday festivities—but there was always some drama too.

Ms. Friedman has written more than forty books for young readers. She is the author of the **Mostly Miserable Life of April Sinclair** series, the award-winning **Mallory** series, and many picture books. She lives in Miami with her family. You can find Laurie B. Friedman on Facebook or visit her on the web at www.lauriebfriedman.com.